THE HOWL OF KANTA

THE WOLVES OF KANTA
BOOK 5

MARLENA FRANK

Edited by: Lara Zielinksy
http://lzedits.com

Cover Art by: Harvest Moon Designs
https://www.facebook.com/groups/HarvestMoonDesigns

Map and Illustrations by: Kelley M. Frank
http://morbidsmile.com

EB ISBN: 978-1-955854-15-3
PB ISBN: 978-1-955854-16-0
HB ISBN: 978-1-955854-17-7

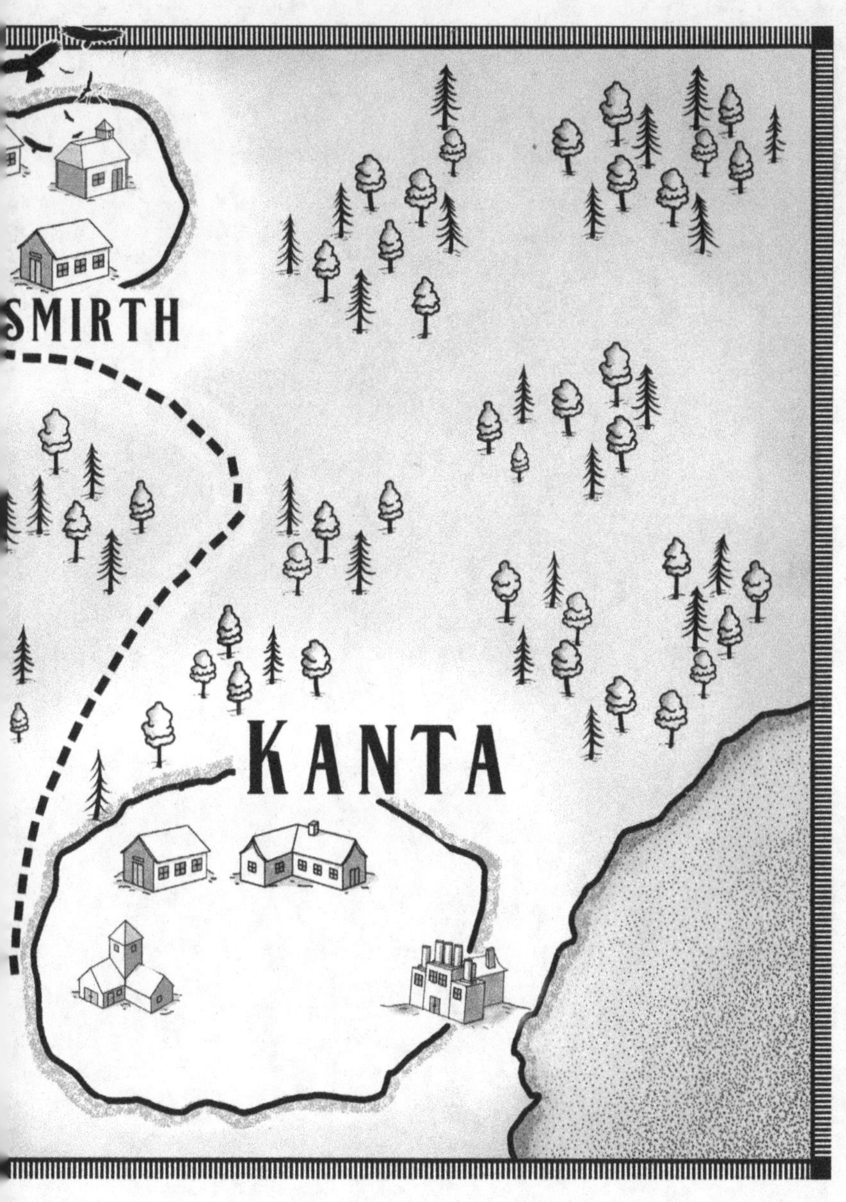

SMIRTH
KANTA

PART 1

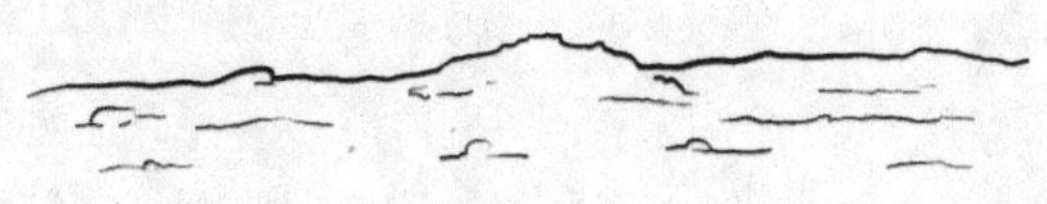

1

———————————

BREAKING IN

HIGH ABOVE MERCY'S HEAD, the stars emerged in the dark sky. Candles and oil lanterns shone golden through the shutters of the houses of Kanta, and the chimneys of Farrell Mill were silent. Mercy had called the mill home for years, working to take care of werewolves there and creating her cure for lycanthropy. It was intimidating when she had first seen it years ago, but now that it was silent, it was haunting.

Farrell Mill usually loomed over Kanta like a mechanical beast with its seven grinders belching steam into the sky. Unlike the rest of town, it never slept. The constant movement was due to the enslaved werewolves at first, but Mercy had convinced Thomas to release them. Now it ran on the gears and pulleys Thomas was so good at building. The ovens in the bellows beneath the building ran constantly hot, powered by coal instead of werewolves. They never went out, so the grinders always turned. The constant rolling roar echoed across Kanta.

Or they used to.

Mercy sat in the dilapidated truck beside Rose, looking to the starry skies for any sign of steam and straining her ears for any grinder. But she was met with silence.

"It looks abandoned," Rose said, her voice low in a hushed whisper.

"That's not possible. The grinders never stop." Mercy's voice shook. Her hands trembled on the dash.

Rose put a hand on her shoulder, giving it a gentle squeeze.

Mercy didn't know much about Rose, only that they had both been held captive at her old family home by a man named Oscar Krim. They had been forced to work for him, though Rose had been there longer than she had. Rose had been his pet werewolf, a housekeeper, and unwilling companion. She had been terrified of him. After Rose got beaten once, after Oscar found them talking, any chance of casual communication had shut down. After that, they didn't risk talking very often, which was probably Oscar's plan all along.

Mercy was kept as the daughter Oscar never had. She had to cook and clean, but Oscar had ways of getting to her head. He had crawled under her skin and, even though he was dead, she thought about him far too often.

Under Oscar's watch, Rose had been chained up every night like a dog. To him, her nightly transformations into a murderous werewolf were an inconvenience. After Mercy worked up the courage to protect herself and kill Oscar, she had finally given Rose the partial cure she needed to get her lycanthropy under control. Together, Rose and Mercy had piled into the truck to reach Farrell Mill, her true home, her sanctuary. Now it, too, was a shadow of its former self, just like her childhood home.

Why couldn't things go the way Mercy planned for once?

"Is there somewhere else we can go?" Rose asked as she looked around at the empty streets. "I may be safe against any werewolves that come hunting, but you won't be."

The question pulled Mercy from her thoughts. She watched Rose look around with a pit of sorrow in her stomach. There was no other place for them to go. Not in Kanta and not in Crowsmirth. They might have better chances going back to Mercy's house and scraping by a living with the two werewolves they left back there permanently changed by the Liquid Lead: Silver and Jamison. But even if that might save her and Rose, it wouldn't save their friends. Thomas, Leyda, and Kit still needed them. And Andrei too…

Mercy unbuckled her seatbelt. "I'm going inside. Wait here."

"What? But how are you going to get in? Do you have a key?"

Mercy hopped out of the truck. As her boots hit the icy ground, she said, "No, but there's a hammer in the back. We'll break in."

Rose's eyes went wide. "That door is metal. Somebody is going to hear you! They'll find us."

"I once saw the sheriff get eaten by a werewolf in

the middle of the night. I'm sure he screamed, but nobody came to help him. I don't think people go out at night in Kanta, even when somebody needs help."

Rose shook her head. "What a strange place. Don't they care about people getting hurt? One dead body could bring dozens of werewolves."

Mercy shook her head. "They don't care about people dying. Not here."

Her boots crunching on the frozen ground, Mercy went to the truck bed and pulled out the hammer. Her fingers froze against the metal handle. In all honesty, she wasn't sure if she could use it to break into the mill, but Rose transforming to tear the door off made her nervous. This was a safer place to die by werewolves than for a werewolf to transform. Someone breaking in somewhere would hardly be news, but a person transforming into a werewolf long after night fell? That was far too risky, even for her.

Mercy approached the front door of the mill, hammer gripped tight. The normal-sized door was part of a much larger metal entrance. When the mill was open during the day, the large door would be left open with guards. Werewolf hunters came to sell their catches to Thomas. These days, Thomas mostly took in werewolves who hadn't been given Liquid Lead so they could cure and re-home them with the partial cure Mercy created. But with the mill closed, she had no idea if those missions were still happening. In fact, she had no idea if Andrei and Kit even made it back to the mill after that horrible day at Crowsmirth when Mercy had been kidnapped by Oscar. The thought of Andrei being out in the woods looking for her made her chest tighten so bad she had to place a palm to her ribs. Her heartbeat thundered under her fingertips.

Calm down.

She couldn't lose it. Not here and not now. Not after surviving so much to get here. There was no point in letting her mind run off in a thousand directions of possibilities. None of that helped her find them. If anything, it would paralyze her to the spot. She reached for the door handle, hoping it would be unlocked. Hoping for the first time in her life she would be lucky. She wrapped a hand around the iron doorknob and pushed.

The door was locked tight. It didn't even rattle on its hinges.

She huffed a puff of air into the cold night air. Nothing was ever easy, certainly not for her.

Everything was solid metal: the door, the handle, even the hinges. It had no windows, no gaps, and no clear signs of weakness where she could pry her way inside. Thomas had built this entrance to keep out werewolves and intruders, and it seemed to work a little too well.

"Try the hinges."

Mercy turned. Rose had come to stand behind her, bundled up against the cold. Beyond her, Main Street was empty, but the shadows felt too dark. Her eyes darted among the pools of darkness. It played tricks on her eyes. She kept seeing movement from the corner of her vision, but when she looked directly, she saw nothing. Were werewolves already approaching in those shadows, or was it just her imagination and paranoia?

"Whatever you do, don't transform here. I don't know if it's safe or not. A break-in is one thing, but if you transform out here, somebody might see something."

Rose held up her hands. "Calm down, I didn't say anything about changing. I'm just trying to help you break in!" She chuckled. "I thought you said people don't care about what happens in the streets at night?"

Mercy shook her head. "This place is full of were-wolf hunters. If you transformed here and someone saw you, they wouldn't come out to get a better look. They would come out to kill the both of us. They would think you're some kind of new breed or something. These people are superstitious, paranoid, and shoot first."

The mirth in Rose's face faded. "I'm not trying to make light of this place. I'm just trying to help with the door. You looked like you needed me."

Mercy pressed a hand hard to her chest to relieve the tension building up inside again. "I'm sorry. I just— my friends are missing. I'm worried about them. This place is my home and I've never seen it abandoned like this." She paused for a moment. "They're more than my friends… they're my family."

Rose gave her a sympathetic nod. "It's okay. I can understand that. Just remember you're not alone. You're as eager to find your family as I am to find Leyda." Worry creased between her brows. "Please. Let me help."

Leyda was Rose's girlfriend, her love. Mercy had

almost forgotten that. Everyone had thought Rose was dead when she wasn't at the werewolf camp the last time they went. Leyda had fallen apart, crying and screaming. She grew even more hostile to Mercy afterward. This was about more than Mercy's family. It was about Rose's family too.

Mercy turned back to the door. "You mentioned the hinges?"

Rose brushed past her to the door. "They're on the outside, which means we can take them apart and the door should fall off. It'll take some time, but if you have something small, you could knock out the hinges with that hammer of yours. Or I could try to pull the door off myself. I think I might have to transform to do that."

Mercy imagined Rose wrenching the door off the wall as a fully transformed werewolf. There was no way that wouldn't attract attention. Honestly, she wasn't sure if Rose even could, considering Thomas built this place specifically to keep werewolves out.

"Let me try it my way first," Mercy said. "I think there were a few nails rattling around in the back of the truck." Having something tangible to focus on helped ease the tension in her chest. She rushed to the truckbed and climbed inside, feeling around along the dirty, cold metal for the thin nails. She tried not to think about all the bloody belongings she had pulled out of the truckbed back in Oscar's shed, or what kind of stains she was dragging her hands over to find the nails. It was hard to see them in the darkness and her fingers were so frozen it was hard to feel anything either, but eventually she found one. She hopped out of the truck and hurried back over to Rose.

"Found one!"

But Rose didn't look at her. Instead, her gaze was focused on the road in the distance. "You better hurry. I smell werewolves."

Mercy looked back at the road. It looked empty still, but knowing Rose could smell them made the shadows more menacing. She shouldn't be surprised werewolves were coming. It was night and only a few months back, Crowsmirth had been crawling with a hundred of them. Without a word, Mercy went for the door. She pushed the end of the nail into the bottom of a hinge and started hammering. The nail was rusty and the hinge sturdy, but after three solid hits, she did see the top of the pin start to lift up.

"Mercy, if they come too close, I may not have a choice but to transform. I know you don't want me to, but I'm not dying in this street and neither are you." Rose braced her legs as though readying for a werewolf to leap on her any minute, lifting her arms up in a protective stance.

Mercy winced, but nodded. The first pin came loose, and she had to pull hard to get it out. Two more to go. She could do this. "I understand," Mercy said as she started on the next hinge.

If Rose transformed, maybe they would get lucky and nobody would see it. Maybe she was worried for no reason. Maybe she was just panicking.

A long, lonesome howl lilted on the wind, sending a chill down Mercy's spine. Living out in the woods with her father since she was a child, she had gotten very good at pinpointing the distance of werewolf howls. This one was very close. Far closer than she liked. She hammered at the second hinge faster, but this one had rust on it that made it tougher to remove.

"I think I can hold them off, at least for a little while," Rose said, sounding nervous. "Give you some time to work."

A second howl joined the first and Rose went silent. Two werewolves. Mercy recalled Andrei struggling to fight off one werewolf back at the inn in Crowsmirth. Rose had only been given the partial vaccine a day or so back. She wouldn't have the strength to fight off two.

Rose must have come to the same conclusion because soon she was at Mercy's side, prying at the pin while Mercy continued hammering on the base of the hinge. Rose didn't say a word, but Mercy could see the terror clearly etched on her face.

The second hinge came loose. Just once more to go. Mercy stood up on her toes to reach the uppermost hinge. It was an awkward angle, but she didn't have a choice. Fingers frozen, she hammered. She kept missing the nail and hitting her fingers, but she couldn't slow down. They had no time left.

Rose tried to get her fingers under the head of the topmost pin, but it was a struggle for her too. She stopped suddenly and drew close.

Her breath was warm against Mercy's ear. "They're here."

Mercy's blood went cold. She turned to look behind them. Stalking toward them were not two, but three werewolves. They were fanned out, almost equidistant from each other, preventing any escape. Mercy gasped, and that tightness came to her chest again. The door was their only option left. Her brain leaped to an observation without her even thinking about it from years of research and taking notes: they were hunting as a pack. Just like the group at Crowsmirth.

Werewolves were solitary hunters. They weren't supposed to be pack hunters. Of course, after Crowsmirth, she ought to toss all her old beliefs about werewolves out the window.

Rose put a hand on Mercy's shoulder, gave it a squeeze, and walked toward the three werewolves. With a growl, she held her arms out in front of her. Her fingers lengthened and claws tore through her fingertips. Blood dripped down her arms, making rivulets that pooled onto the dirt road. Fur sprouted through her skin as her sleeves ripped to pieces. Soon her fully transformed werewolf arms hung down to her knees as Rose puffed hot cloudy breaths into the cold night air.

The lengthening of her arms and transformation clearly shocked the werewolves. The middle one took a step back from her. The other two didn't seem as frightened. In fact, they seemed incensed, snarling and baring their fangs. Perhaps Rose was seen as a competitor now. One of their own posing as prey.

Mercy got back up on her toes and focused on the final hinge. It seemed foolish to not have Rose use her strength to pull the door off of its frame now, but Mercy knew the terror of the townspeople come morning might be more dangerous than three werewolves attacking them. She didn't want anything to happen to her friend. Not again.

The pin popped up finally and Mercy had to stretch her arm up to pull it out of the hinge. Her fingers sore, she yanked at the stubborn pin. Behind her came sounds of a scuffle. Mercy didn't dare look back. As the pin fell into her hand, she grabbed the door handle quickly to keep it from falling. She dragged the heavy metal door to the side, just enough to slip through.

"Rose, come on!" she cried.

Even though she desperately wanted to turn back and see if Rose was even alive, she instead squeezed her body through the space. It was a tight squeeze, but she made it. The stillness that greeted her inside the cold entrance hall arrested her. She had never seen the mill look so empty, not in the years she had called it home. It reminded her of a tomb more than a factory. Panic rose into her heart when she thought of Andrei, but she pushed it away. She had to focus. Andrei wasn't running from a trio of werewolves. She and Rose were.

She turned back and saw one of the werewolves get flung against the truck, which wobbled on its tires. Then the victor came toward the entrance. Mercy backed away. It was a fully transformed werewolf.

With a whimper, Mercy ran through the chamber, her footfalls echoing across the metal floor. The thumping sound behind her meant one of them had already gotten inside. Her heart thudded in her chest as she sprinted for the door that led to the catwalk of the first grinder.

"Mercy, wait!" A distorted voice called to her.

She warred with herself on if she should stop. If Rose had gotten hurt, she would need help. Then again, Mercy had no chance against those werewolves. She had no weapons, not even a gun or a set of electric prongs. Eventually, her conscience won out.

She stopped and turned back, her legs jittery as she prepared herself to leap into action if needed.

Behind her, several paces back, was Rose. On all fours, blood seeped from her pores. Fur retracted, claws receded, and she left puddles of blood in her path. Soon she had human eyes instead of those of a wolf. Rose had run for the door, only she must have had to fully transform to be able to fight the three werewolves at all.

She hadn't been ready for so much transforming. She had only been given the partial cure a day or so ago. Her body wasn't ready for so much stress on it. Judging by the claw marks on her face and arms, the bite mark on her side, and the way she was panting, she hadn't won that match. She had barely scraped by with her life. The torso of her shirt and top of her pants were barely hanging together, but at least she wasn't fully naked in the frigid factory.

Mercy was at her side in an instant.

"Come on," she urged. Looping one of Rose's arms over her shoulders, she hauled her to her feet. "We can't stop. That door won't keep them back for long."

Rose nodded, trying to help, but she was sluggish. "I shouldn't have done that," she admitted. "I panicked. I should have listened to you and held off on transforming. I should have been helping you with the door instead. I'm sorry."

"It's okay," Mercy said as they made their way up to the door.

A loud, metallic clang jerked Mercy's attention back to the entrance. The heavy metal door had been cast aside. A werewolf stood in the doorway. The moon cast its shadow across the floor. The beast tilted its head back and howled in victory, cold breath steaming out of its throat. The others joined in behind them, creating a cacophony of noise that echoed through the metal room.

Mercy hissed in pain as her ears rang. Rose gritted her teeth against it. Together they hobbled to the wooden door that led to the first grinder. Mercy yanked open the door and closed it behind them. The bitter cold greeted them as snow fell softly from the dark sky.

Rose looked around with wide eyes at the catwalk ahead of them and the long distance to the ground. "Mercy, we're easy prey up here! I was hoping we would at least find a place to hide."

Mercy led her wordlessly to the ladder. "Climb down," she said.

Rose stared at her with wide, fearful eyes.

"Don't ask, just do it. Trust me."

Clenching her jaw, Rose started climbing, but not without giving Mercy a look as if she had lost her mind.

In all honesty, Mercy wasn't sure if this would work, but she refused to lead the werewolves back to the tower and possibly back to her friends. If this grinder could keep werewolves inside, then maybe it could keep them out, too.

Even injured, Rose made quick work of the ladder.

Mercy's arms were burning before she was even halfway down. It was hard to believe she used to climb up and down these with ease just months back. Living with Oscar had impacted her body more than she realized. She had just hit the snowy ground when the sound of splintering wood made her heart leap into her throat. She looked up to the base of the catwalk and heard their claws clicking on the metal. Snow drifted down from the guardrails, unsettled by their movements. The werewolves were directly above them.

Walking slowly, Mercy winced as her boots crunched in the icy snow. She half-expected to see one of the werewolves leap down beside her, but they didn't. Rose was hidden beneath the catwalk, close to the wall. She sat in the snow, clearly too exhausted to stand. Still, she gestured for Mercy to join her, fear etched on her face.

Mercy didn't hurry, she took her time. That was the best option to keep from attracting their attention.

They were pacing up above, probably trying to catch their scent. They would figure it out eventually. Werewolves, she knew, had an incredible sense of smell. They could smell humans from miles away. They would figure out where they were. Once they did, Mercy wasn't sure what they would do.

She finally reached Rose, who pulled her down into the snow beside her and wrapped Mercy in a warm embrace. Rose had tears in her eyes. Mercy had no idea what all Oscar did to Rose in her time serving him, or even how Rose was bitten and turned into a werewolf. But she imagined all of this only made things worse. Mercy had hoped bringing her here would be an escape, a rest after the violence they had seen, but it wasn't. Mercy hated her own fear of Kanta had led them to this point. If they could have existed comfortably in Kanta during the day like all the hunters did, they wouldn't have had to get here at night. They wouldn't be fighting off werewolves. They could have come back to the mill, found a way inside, and be safe from the werewolves hours ago. Mercy hated that Kanta made everything so difficult for them.

A howl pulled her from her thoughts. She looked up and suspected they were crowded around one spot: the ladder. That would give them away and tell the wolves exactly where they went.

Suddenly something was flying through the air, big and covered in fur. Mercy gasped. One of them had flung itself over the edge in a desperate attempt to reach them.

The werewolf thought it would land on its feet, but then it twisted wrong at the last minute. She closed her eyes, unable to watch. The crunch of bones made her cringe. Rose squeezed her harder and breathed faster. Mercy opened her eyes and saw its body sat motionless. Snowfall collected on its fur, but it was clearly no longer breathing.

Rose put a hand to her mouth. "Why?" she whispered.

Mercy pursed her lips. It was a good question and she wished she had time to investigate it. Instead, she was too busy trying to survive. She thought of the werewolves that had attacked Kit at her home, willing to hurt themselves on the electric fence for the betterment of the pack. The ones who had attacked Crowsmirth that long night who seemed to coordinate their attack to work together. Now these would kill themselves for a small chance at food. They were far more vicious and pack-oriented than the ones Mercy used to hunt with her father.

She had her suspicions why they were like this. It would also explain their numbers skyrocketing at Crowsmirth. It felt like someone was trying to create an army. Knowing what she did about the people living in Kanta and Crowsmirth, she was certain someone would be cruel enough to do it. The part she hadn't solved yet was why. If only she had time to solve the mystery she would. But right now her friends—no, her family was more important than anything. She would have to let someone else solve it for once. She had more important matters to deal with.

"Do you think they're leaving?" Rose whispered.

Mercy stared at the base of the catwalk. Neither of the other two had leaped off. They were smart. At least smart enough to have some level of self-preservation.

She shook her head at Rose's question. "They're learning." Even saying the words out loud sent a chill down her spine. Werewolves learning how to hunt and kill more efficiently in wolf form was truly the stuff of nightmares. Yet here was the reality staring her in the face.

Two back feet looped into a pair of rungs on the ladder. Mercy's jaw dropped. Surely they weren't coordinated enough to use ladders? The big, burly werewolf seemed determined to prove her wrong. It took its time, somehow squeezing its paw in over each rung. The back feet had more trouble than the front, but it was making progress. Already it was a fifth of the way down.

"We need to get out of here," Mercy said.

"I know, but where do we go? We're trapped down here!" Clear from the waver in Rose's voice, she was starting to panic. That didn't help either of them.

Looking around the grinder, Mercy felt that same panic start to come in on the edges, trying to take over. She had to force it back, but it took effort. Then her gaze fell on something unexpected. A crow stood on one of the ledges that stuck out of the wall. It was pecking at something metal.

Ting—ting—ting!

How had she not noticed it? It was a loud sound, but she was so focused on the werewolves she hadn't noticed it. The crow cocked its head to the side and gave a little caw. A pale hand reached out from the ledge and gestured for them to come. Mercy scrambled to her feet.

"Rose, come on, we have to hurry!" She didn't even try to be quiet this time. What was the point? They already knew where they were.

Rose hauled herself up to her feet slowly and followed.

Mercy had helped clean the grinders for months when she first came to the mill. It wasn't easy work and mostly involved scrubbing the drainage holes for algae and mold. The space was far too small for a werewolf, but it might fit two people. That felt like it had happened a lifetime ago.

A howl made Mercy's heart leap into her throat. She

glanced to the catwalk and saw that the werewolf at the top had spotted them. The one on the ladder dropped a couple of rungs and almost fell. He was over halfway down. They were running out of time.

When they reached the far wall, Mercy jumped up to reach the drainage ledge, but she couldn't jump that high. They had harnesses and equipment to help lower them down from the top when they cleaned the grinders. Without that, without safety, it would be harder. She tried again, jumping less high than before.

"Let me help," Rose said. She linked her hands together to give Mercy a boost up. Mercy stepped up. If Rose wasn't a werewolf, she probably wouldn't have been able to lift her so high. Mercy's jump this time with Rose's help, almost overshot the ledge and she had to grab onto it.

As the crow flew off, Kit smiled at Mercy from behind the metal grating. Her face was grimy with dirt and her black hair hung limply in her face, but her eyes shone with excitement. Without a word, she lifted the metal grate up and back. Then she climbed out and took Mercy's hand to pull her inside.

"Hang on, one more!" Mercy cried.

Kit nodded and held the grate up as Mercy turned and reached out over the ledge. Rose jumped, got hold of Mercy's hand with a grunt, and just got her other hand onto the ledge as the werewolf on the ladder dropped to the ground. It started running for them at a sprint, mouth open and fangs bared. The werewolf on the catwalk howled again.

Mercy helped Rose up to the ledge and pulled her

into the drainage pipe. Between the three of them, it was a tight squeeze, but they fit. Kit reached up to push the grate forward and closed just as a werewolf paw reached up to grab onto the ledge. While it had taken Mercy and Rose a bit to climb up to the ledge, the werewolf pulled itself up without any trouble.

Kit latched the base of the grate just in time. The werewolf linked its long fingers through the grate and its sharp nails scraped against the metal as it snarled at them. Thick saliva dripped down from its yellowed fangs. Heat from its breath mixed with a familiar rancid smell and Mercy crawled backwards away from it. Rose was kneeing her in the thigh in her urgency to turn and crawl back farther into the drainage pipe.

Mercy was transfixed by the werewolf. Its golden eyes glinted in the moonlight, glowing with an inner light. No intelligence enlivened its eyes like she had seen in the ones at Oscar's compound. She saw only fierce hunger and cruel determination. Snow had settled on its shoulders as it tried to shove its nose through the grate and it sniffed the air, more saliva dripping down. Then it snarled and rattled the grate again.

"This way!" Kit called to them. Her voice bounced along the metal shaft. Mercy tore her gaze over her shoulder. Kit was yards away from her. Where did this pipe empty out? Despite living in Farrell Mill for years, Mercy didn't recall anything about these pipes. Rose scrambled down the pipe on her hands and knees. Mercy turned back to the werewolf who was trying to bite through the metal. This space was made to keep werewolves out and Mercy knew that metal was too dense for them to get their teeth through it. Their claws could do some damage, but normally their bites could break bone. The werewolf couldn't get good purchase with its teeth. The grate design was simple but surprisingly effective.

"Mercy!" Rose hissed.

She jumped and turned so she could follow Rose and Kit down the pipe. "I'm coming!"

The pipe angled slightly down, easing the flow of water that sometimes filled the grinder during downpours or heavy snowfall. But it wasn't so steep that it was impossible to climb up or down. Behind them Mercy heard the continued snarling and snapping of the angry werewolf, but as they took one turn, then another, following the path water would take, the sounds grew more and more faint until all she could hear was their breathing and the padding of their hands and knees across the piping. Some areas were slippery from a buildup of algae, but Mercy would rather deal with that instead of the werewolf.

It didn't take long for Mercy's hands to freeze. Her fingers were still throbbing from dealing with the metal door hinges. But other than the throbbing pain, she couldn't feel much else. However, she didn't say a word of complaint. None of them did. Mercy had no idea what they were crawling near or who might be nearby. She didn't want to risk anything, not after barely escaping with their lives.

They came to a crossroads of five pipes all meeting together. A pipe in the middle went straight down.

"Be careful here," Kit whispered.

Mercy could barely see her in the dim light, but she heard the worry in her voice. Once again, Mercy wondered what had happened to the mill. What had happened to Thomas and Leyda, and most importantly, where the hell was Andrei?

Kit put her hands out to the other pipes as she stood in a crouch, careful to step around the exit pipe. Then she pulled herself up into another pipe seemingly at random compared to the other equally dark pipes.

Shaking from head to toe, Rose stood up slowly. This was far too much exertion for someone who had just fully transformed and had been beaten up by three werewolves. When Andrei had fought off one werewolf after fully transforming, he had passed out in a broom closet. Mercy was worried Rose would also be tempted to pass out, but that was too dangerous to do here. So Mercy stood up carefully, bracing her arm around Rose's waist.

"Be careful. You don't want to fall."

"Thank you, Mercy." Rose gave her a smile. "I just feel wiped is all." Claw marks glistened across her cheek, red and inflamed. They should be better healed by now, but Rose hadn't been given time to recover. She hadn't had the chance to even eat anything, which was a requirement. Transformations took a lot of exertion and a lot of energy. Not to mention the pain she had to be in scurrying around in freezing, dark pipes wearing mere scraps of clothing.

"It's okay, I've got you," Mercy said, keeping Rose from falling as Kit reached over to help her up into the pipe. Once Rose was resting up ahead at a bend, Kit turned to Mercy.

"Looks like they cut her up pretty bad. The path into the tower is just past this pipe, but it's all uphill. Is she going to be okay?"

Mercy took a breath. Her arms and legs were sore, her entire body ached, and she was exhausted, but she gave a nod. "I'll go after her and make sure she doesn't fall. If we work together, she'll be okay." Mercy lowered her voice, looking toward the pipe where Rose rested. "Is Leyda nearby? Maybe we could get her help. I'm sure she wants to see Rose."

Kit bit her lip. "No, she's not here. I don't really know where she went. I wish she stayed, but it got too dangerous. I mean, I don't blame her, but I could use her help."

Mercy wanted to press her for more information, but Kit moved on to the pipe to help Rose. She hadn't said anything about Andrei. Why? She hadn't mentioned a word about Mercy disappearing at Crowsmirth. Did she think Mercy had abandoned her like Leyda? She felt a heat raise up to her neck and cheeks as frustration pricked over her. This wasn't the time for answers. They had to get to safety first. That was more important than knowledge. For now, at least.

Mercy put her hands onto the curvature of the various pipes, her hands freezing all over again. She had finally started getting them warmer. With a sigh, she took careful steps around the bottom pipe. Distantly she heard the sounds of winter night, a howling wind, and the occasional iciness of steady snowfall. She caught the scent of snow and pine and it made her momentarily wish she had stayed at her childhood home. It wasn't the best place, but at least it was safe. At least there was food and shelter. Maybe they should have stayed longer. At least until winter had passed.

Her boots crunched down on some lingering ice on the next pipe. Kit had rushed ahead. Mercy wasn't sure if it was to avoid talking to her more or if it was just to lead the way out of the pipes.

It was probably the latter. Frustration pricked at her, saying otherwise, but Mercy knew that wasn't the truth. Either way, she promised herself that soon she would have answers.

2

FREEZING UP

THE FINAL PIPE was steeper than the others, and it was a struggle to climb up. The slippery algae that had gathered on the metal didn't help. It was even more challenging climbing while helping Rose.

Rose did well enough at first, but she quickly ran out of steam the longer the climb continued. Mercy didn't blame her. Rose had been so helpful on their journey back to Kanta and escaping those three werewolves Mercy wasn't sure if she would have made it back on her own. Rose had fought for her, even moved trees for her. Mercy could deal with a little discomfort in helping her escape these pipes.

Up ahead, Mercy spotted a flickering light. Her entire body ached at the sight of it. Only a little further to go. When she caught the acrid scent of lantern oil, immediately she knew where they were. They were inside the laboratory at the base of the tower. This was where all the werewolves were kept that she had cared for, fed meat to, changed soiled hay for, and, in later years, experimented on. A swell of emotion built up inside as she took in the scent of oil.

It wasn't just a laboratory. Not anymore. This was her home. A place where she felt not only safe, but where her abilities and ideas had value. A place where she could spend hours focusing on her experiments or poring over research notes without judgment or restrictions. Tears came to her eyes and her heart beat faster. She had no words for how much the space meant to her or how much she missed it. Worse yet, she hadn't realized how much she missed it until she smelled it.

After several long minutes, they finally climbed through a hole in the corner of the room where a grate used to be. Mercy hadn't really noticed the drainage site before, but she was incredibly grateful for now.

Pushing off the cold stone floor, she climbed to her feet. She looked around the room at all the werewolf cages and the many amber eyes that looked back at her. She wasn't just home; she was here again with her friends. Every single werewolf she knew and cared for. Even the one she and her father had brought in years ago that had clawed her in the back.

Tears streamed down Mercy's cheeks as she went between each of the cages, reaching in to take fur-clad paws and the occasionally nuzzling snout.

"I'm so sorry I left all of you," Mercy said through a constricted throat as she greeted them all. "I didn't want to leave you. I didn't mean to abandon you. I promise." She got back to where Kit stood and where Rose was slumped on the floor. Kit watched her with wide, worried eyes.

"What happened to you?" Kit asked.

Mercy shook her head and pulled Kit into a tight embrace, unable to speak. Kit hugged her back, seeming startled, though she slowly hugged her tighter. Eventually Mercy pulled back and stared into Kit's eyes. She was covered in grime, as though she had been scurrying around in those tunnels for a very long time. She looked thin, like she hadn't been eating. Her eyes were sunken in as though sleep had evaded her for too many nights. But why? What had happened to everyone?

"A hunter captured me," Mercy said, gaining control over her voice again. "He kidnapped me. Rose was already his prisoner when he brought me in."

"He was a sadistic loony, if you ask me," Rose chimed in, still breathing hard. "That man got a real kick out of torturing people. I thought he only liked to torment werewolves until Mercy came along." She glanced over at Mercy. "Don't get me wrong, I was grateful you were there, but I wouldn't have wanted anyone to have to deal with Oscar the way we did. A violent hunter of a man if I ever saw one."

Kit slid a cool hand into Mercy's palm. "He didn't hurt you, did he, Mercy?"

The tremor in her voice broke Mercy's heart.

She had to stop to consider. Oscar had caged her, trapped her inside her childhood home. He had threatened to shoot and kill her many times, and he had struck her on more than one occasion. Mostly though, he took his anger out on Rose. He had used her as his personal punching bag to keep Mercy in line. And it had worked.

Oscar never hurt her as much as he did Rose.

Looking back, she wondered if perhaps it was because he wanted her to see him as a father figure instead of the monster he was. Or perhaps he was trying to be a better father than her real father had been, as if that had ever been possible.

"He struck me," Mercy said, putting a hand to her cheek as she remembered that first night back at her childhood home. Oscar had seemed almost as surprised that he hit her as she was. Instead of the bruise though, Mercy felt scars from the claw marks Rose had given her as a transformed werewolf. She shook her head. "But it was nothing like what he put Rose through."

Rose's bitter laugh caught Mercy off guard. "Sure, he hurt me more physically, but I think at the end, you were a little convinced he could be a father to you. He got his claws dug deep into you. He hurt you psychologically far worse than you think."

Mercy blinked. "No, that's not true!"

"You couldn't even shoot him at the end!" Rose said, bitterness lacing her words. "And I know you tried."

Mercy winced as a weight fell in her stomach.

"She had a loaded gun aimed at the man's head and she couldn't pull the trigger," Rose told Kit. Her voice trembled with a mixture of exhaustion and rage. "He had you under his thumb," she continued, looking back at Mercy, "whether you want to admit it or not. If I hadn't been there, I bet he would still have a hold over you. He wanted to turn you into a twisted version of himself."

Mercy shook from head to toe, unable to bring herself to deny it. Had she allowed Oscar to get under her skin that badly? Had she almost allowed him to turn her into his daughter, a version of himself? The very thought repulsed her.

"It all happened so fast," Mercy whispered, her voice breaking. "I didn't mean for—I never wanted that —" That wasn't entirely true. She liked feeling needed, being useful to someone. It was what had defined most of her life growing up with her father. Her worth had always been linked to being useful. That was one of the reasons she had wanted to prove herself to Thomas so badly, and what ultimately led to the creation of the partial cure for lycanthropy. That was also clearly a weakness that Oscar tried to use against her. She thought she had resisted Oscar better than that. But Rose was right. She had refused to shoot him. She couldn't bring herself to do it. Maybe with a little more time, a little more isolation, and a little less determination, she could have found herself assisting a true monster.

She couldn't ever let herself fall into that trap again. She couldn't allow herself to be used like that.

"I'm not trying to be mean," Rose said. "Maybe I'm just tired. Maybe that's it." She looked at her with concern in her eyes. "I'm sorry, Mercy. You helped me down there and I'm being a jerk. You don't deserve that."

Trembling, Mercy lifted her head to meet Rose's gaze. "No, don't be sorry. I needed to hear this. I need to know, so I can prevent it. I won't know any better unless I know what my weaknesses are. It hurts, but you're right. Oscar got to me more than I like to admit. Maybe even more than I realized." She swiped away her spilled tears. "I've been so busy surviving and just trying to get by every day that I forget to stop and listen. To learn, so I don't get taken advantage of again. So thank you for that."

Kit squeezed Mercy's hand, her palms rough against her skin. "You're both tired and probably need to sleep before we plan our next step. Mercy has her old room upstairs. Rose, maybe you could use—"

"No!" Mercy shook her head and shook Kit's hand, gripping it so tight her knuckles blanched. Kit stared at her with shock. "I can't sleep yet. I need to know where Andrei is. I mean—" She closed her eyes, tried to focus, but all she could see was Andrei's face. Thankfully, Kit understood the words she couldn't seem to get out.

"You mean—where Thomas, Leyda, and Andrei are?"

"Yes!" she cried, smiling even though she caught the lack of joy in Kit's voice, the lack of amusement in her eyes. She hadn't found Mercy's struggle with words funny, which meant this was serious. It meant whatever had happened to them had been serious. That tightness in her chest returned with a vengeance.

"They're not here."

Mercy gasped. "Not here? What do you mean? Are they hiding down in the bellows or something?" She laughed, but no mirth came out.

"Mercy, the bellows haven't been running for months, not since Farrell Mill was shut down."

"Shut down—wait, you're not making any sense. They can't shut the mill down. Leyda and Andrei would have nowhere else to go. This is their home. Plus, the people of Kanta rely on the mill to sell werewolves. It's how they make money here. They wouldn't shut it down."

She froze for a moment as a horrible thought came to her, one that had been fluttering about in the back of her mind ever since they drove up and saw Farrell Mill was dark and the chimneys empty of steam. "Unless..."

Kit pursed her lips and gave a short nod, pulling her hand away from Mercy's grip. "Unless they found out what was going on behind the scenes and then jumped to their own assumptions about the rest."

Mercy stared at her as a coldness spread across her fingers. Her heart pounded harder in her chest, the tightness there unbearable. She put a hand to her chest, warding it off, pushing it down, pushing it back.

"Farrell Mill was closed down the day the sheriff raided it and arrested Thomas and Andrei. They're down at the jail and supposedly went to trial today. I didn't dare go to see how it went, but it couldn't have gone well." Kit folded her arms, looking small and sad in the great chamber of the laboratory. "They were cheering in the streets that day after they were arrested."

Mercy only vaguely heard Rose ask about Leyda. Her head was spinning too fast, her breathing too rapid, and the world didn't feel real any longer.

"I don't know," Kit said, her eyes downcast as she chewed on her lip. "I didn't think she was here when they raided the mill, but she closed the door to the laboratory while I was down here. The only way I could get out was through the drainage tunnels. There was...

shooting. I don't know what happened. I'm sorry, Rose, but I haven't seen her since."

———————

THE COOL SHEETS were soft against her freshly washed skin. The snow outside fell heavily, but the small fireplace in Mercy's bedroom kept her warm against the howling wind. It was easily the most comfortable bed she had slept in for months and her entire body was leaden with sleep, but her eyes simply wouldn't close. Her mind hadn't stopped churning since she heard the news from Kit about what had happened to Thomas and her poor Andrei.

Every time she tried to doze off to sleep, she thought of Andrei locked up in that disgusting jail that smelled of old urine and feces. The place smelled so bad Leyda hadn't been able to step inside to sign some paperwork. Mercy thought of Andrei trying to sleep in that place for months and her heart broke again and again.

She thought of his kind smile, warm hands, and soft lips. She cried until she wasn't sure she had any tears left. She screamed into her pillow and beat her fists against the mattress. It wasn't fair. They were supposed to be happy together. Andrei was supposed to have been waiting for her to return, to escape. The people of Kanta had taken their perfect reunion away from them.

Thomas? Yeah, he probably deserved to get locked up for a few months. He had done some truly horrible things in the past, like tearing off the arms of werewolves and using them as manual labor. She had to give him credit for trying to make up for his past mistakes, but he had never been punished for any of that. He had never seen any kind of consequences that she knew of. So while she was upset he was locked up, it seemed at least somewhat fair, considering what he had done.

Andrei, on the other hand, was completely innocent. He had been the only survivor after his entire family was slaughtered by werewolves. Then he volunteered to be a guard for his werewolf camp out in the woods, protecting them from hunters. Now he was living in a rancid jail cell, all because Mercy needed to find a volunteer to be experimented on by Thomas. He came back to the laboratory and agreed to be experimented on because he liked her. He would never have suggested it, but Mercy knew she was the reason he was even in this mess. Now he was in a jail cell.

Outside, the moon peeked through a cloudy sky. It was late in the evening and Mercy knew she needed to rest if she was going to be useful to anyone tomorrow.

She stretched to reach the bedside table and ate the last of the stale bread left from dinner, and downed the remainder of her water. With food on her stomach, she curled up under the blankets and stared up at the moon making her silver path across the sky.

"Tomorrow, Andrei, I'm going to figure out a way to get you home to me safe. I hope you're okay. I hope they aren't hurting you. I don't care how many walls we have to tear down or people we have to shove aside to do it. I will see you again. We will be together. I promise."

She yawned and started to doze off. Her mind returned to a conversation she had with Oscar a few months back. They were checking traps on the perimeter of the property, looking for any animals that had been captured.

"Two squirrels! Looks like one got trapped, and the other died trying to rescue them. Couple of foolish creatures. So hellbent on saving someone they died."

In her dream, Oscar kept laughing while Mercy stared down in horror as the two squirrels morphed into her and Andrei, dead and motionless, facing each other as they took their last breaths.

Even in death, their hands were apart, unable to reach each other until it no longer mattered.

Oscar laughed with horrid joy. "Squirrels."

A SLAMMING door jolted Mercy awake. Her eyes shot open as heavy footfalls creaked on the wooden floorboards. Somebody had entered the tower. They were floors below her, but the sound of that door was buried deep in her unconsciousness.

In her drowsy panic, it took her a moment to realize where she was and why her body was screaming at her to move. No, she wasn't at home. The floors in her house had a different creaking sound. It wasn't Oscar; he was dead. Not Thomas or Andrei; they were in jail. So why were the hairs on her arms standing on end?

The footsteps moved slowly, trying not to let the wood creak again. More than one, they spoke in low voices, trying to be quiet. That meant they didn't want to be heard. That wasn't a good sign. That meant she was in danger. Whoever it was, she needed to hide. She needed to move.

Mercy jumped to her feet, icy coldness shooting up her feet from the freezing floor. The fire in the fireplace had gone out, leaving the room too cold. She needed to hide, but where? She considered hiding under the bed, the only other available place, but that was too obvious. It was the only place in the room where she could fit. She glanced at the window, but she had no idea if the windows even opened up to the outside.

Mercy suddenly remembered Mitchell having to be her nursemaid while she was sick in this room, shortly after Thomas and Leyda had found her in the woods and brought her back. Mitchell had to wring wet towels out of that window—which meant they did open!

She pulled on her clothes haphazardly and stuffed her feet into her boots. After getting dressed, she pulled the blankets off the bed and secured them around her waist. She hauled the comforter over her shoulders and went for the window. A needlessly complicated mechanism in true Thomas fashion, Mercy knew his methods well. She stepped out of the window and onto the thin ledge, grateful for the extra layers of warmth from the blankets and comforter.

Cold wind bit into her bare skin as she stood on the ledge that was only a foot or so wide. She pulled the window closed behind her, unable to latch it, but at least she got it to close. The ledge circled around the edge of the tower, which meant she had plenty of space to move to the side and around the rounded wall. It would allow her to be hidden from view if they looked out the window. She just needed to keep her balance and not fall.

She swallowed down her fear as she glanced down at the sheer drop. Taking a deep breath, she inched her way around the wall, holding onto the metal grating of the tower, her fingers clutching the edges of the rivets.

When the door to her bedroom slammed open, Mercy's heart leaped to her throat. She jumped instinctively and almost lost her balance, but caught it back again. Breathing hard, she leaned her head against the metal wall, cold against her forehead. Several pairs of footsteps echoed from her room as they checked it. She strained her ears to see if she could figure out what was going on.

"Sheriff Barlow? The embers are still warm."

Damn, she had forgotten about the fireplace. Her instincts had saved her when it came to the blankets and her clothes, but she hadn't considered the fireplace.

"Could be the rogue werewolf or the two suspects that eyewitnesses spotted last night. You saw that vehicle, Lieutenant Hastings, dented in on the side. Whoever they are, they are clearly Farrell sympathizers. Why else would they choose to break into such a fortified building instead of going to the jail or any other safe place to hide from a werewolf attack? That's not what innocent people do. That's the sign of someone who's guilty. It seems fishy to me."

Mercy slid another foot along the ledge, trying to put as much distance between her and them as she could.

"Word says that truck was stolen years ago from

some hunter up north. Then there's that weird painting…" Hastings said.

"Keep your voice down!" The sheriff hissed. "Remember that painting is off the books until we get more information on it."

"Sorry, sir. It's just a puzzle, is all. I feel like the more I try to unravel, the less sense it all makes."

Barlow laughed. "Welcome to Kanta, Lieutenant."

"What about Farrell and his assistant down in the jail? Did they say anything when you interrogated them this morning?"

Mercy leaned to the side, shifting her feet so she could get a better angle to hear. They were talking about Thomas and Andrei. She needed to know what they were dealing with.

"Not a damn word. Even the kid had no reaction, no matter what I did. And that Farrell has a pain tolerance like none I've seen. Twisted his fingers around first thing this morning and he screamed in pain—but it was almost like he was acting. That one's a real whack-job. I don't trust anything he says. Though they have both been very quiet since the verdict came down from the judge yesterday."

Mercy dug her fingers into the grooves of the metal, leaning forward to hear, her heart thudding so hard in her chest that it felt like it could burst through her ribcage.

"What did the judge say, anyway? Surely they're not innocent!" Hastings scoffed. "I had too many friends weaseled by their scam of buying werewolves. He always said he gave them a shoddy deal, but I never imagined he was reselling them elsewhere. He's been doing this for decades. It's disgusting."

"You'll learn soon enough, Hastings, that the corruption on the streets of Kanta knows no depths. But the judge is thankfully a wise man. He ordered that those two by shot to death by a firing squad in three days' time."

The world spun around Mercy as the sheriff's words sank in. Her Andrei shot to death in a public space? Oh no, they would find out he wasn't fully human. They would kill him. They would destroy him. Oh no. The very thought of Andrei lying dead in a pool of his own blood settled the cold over her like a frozen shawl. She clamped her teeth together to keep from crying out. From making any sound. She had to keep her head. She had to tell the others. Her poor Andrei.

"Even the kid?" Lieutenant Hastings asked. "Seems a little harsh, don't you think, sir?"

"Oh, he may be a teenager, but don't forget the monster he helped. If he was set free, what is to keep him from coming back and taking up the mantle of his old boss all over again? You have to think about these things, Lieutenant. If he's old enough to help a monster like Farrell, he's old enough to dig up his own trouble."

"I don't know, sir. There's a big gap between killing someone and letting them take up this kind of work again. There has to be some kind of middle ground somewhere."

More of the sheriff's nauseating laughter rang in Mercy's ears. "See, that's the exact attitude that's going to get you killed one day. If you go soft on these criminals, they will walk all over you! It doesn't matter what age they are, they're all accomplices in the eyes of the law. And you represent that law now, my good man. It's your job to enforce it."

Hastings was silent a moment. "If you say so, sir."

Shifting backwards, Mercy suddenly wanted to put as much space as possible between herself and these two. She was starting to tremble and that could get her killed if she wasn't careful, staring down at the long distance between her and the base of one of the grinders way below. Something shifted under her back foot, possibly a large piece of gravel or a piece of metal that had fallen from the top of the tower. Either way, Mercy had to stand on one foot hundreds of feet above the ground on a ledge that was far too small. In her panic, she kicked the metal piece off the ledge, sending it clattering noisily to the ground below. She cringed as she regained her balance, listening as it hit the wall again and again with a loud clamber.

"Hold up," Barlow hissed. "Did you hear that?"

"Sure did, sir. Where did it come from?"

Mercy shuffled back along the ledge as quick as she could. Only the ledge didn't circle around the entire tower like she expected it to. She looked backward to see a drop off behind her back foot and was reminded that she didn't even have her boots properly tied. Not that she had the ability or the space to tie them now.

"Sounded like it came from out here," Barlow said.

The window to her bedroom opened. Mercy froze as she spotted a gray head of hair and a bushy mustache belonging to a man with pale blue eyes and a cold expression just visible behind the curve of the tower.

"Sir? Anything?" Lieutenant Hastings asked from inside the room.

"No, not a damn thing." The sheriff shook his head.

Mercy was shaking so badly, it felt like they might hear her breathing. A few beads of sweat slid down her back and into her shirt, tied tight with the blankets around her waist.

All the sheriff had to do was turn his head to the left and he would see her. He would spot a terrified teen huddled in bedsheets and blankets, with a comforter slung over her shoulders, getting covered in snow, crouched down on the farthest end of a very precarious ledge. He would probably laugh. Thinking she was the straggler werewolf they were still hunting, he might just shoot her on sight without asking a single question. Of course, if they found out who she really was and who she worked for, they might drag her into a jail cell to rot alongside Thomas and Andrei.

A part of her thought about purposely getting caught, just so she could see Andrei again and make sure he was alive. Quickly she pushed that wild thought away. She couldn't help him escape if she was locked up.

Instead, she crouched as still as a statue, her thighs burning in protest, and all the while hoping her blanket wasn't flapping in the breeze and the platform beneath her feet wouldn't crumble to pieces. She tried her best to not move, to not shake, and to stay as still as a gargoyle.

He glanced to the right and down over the ledge as if she would have even survived that fall. He froze and

Mercy's heart pounded harder, making it difficult to keep her breathing calm and controlled.

"Lieutenant!" he cried, gesturing wildly behind him. "Come here. Look at this." He pointed down at the snow and ice that had collected on the ledge. "What does that look like to you?"

Lieutenant Hastings emerged, a younger man with brown hair and freckles, ruddy cheeks, and strong jaw.

"Snow?"

The sheriff cried out in frustration. "Yes, but what is in the snow?"

"Markings, maybe from a bird?"

"Or shoes."

Lieutenant Hastings cocked his head to the side. "I don't really see it, sir." He caught the sheriff's narrowed eyes. "But if you see it, then that is definitely what it is."

"You need to get your eyes checked." Sheriff Barlow huffed, shaking his head at him. "I think our werewolf quarry jumped ship when we came inside the tower. Jumped to the ground and ran as fast as they could out of this place."

"You think they jumped? Isn't that a long drop, even for a werewolf? I didn't think they would survive that."

"Werewolves aren't people, Lieutenant. They're animals. Remember that."

Mercy knew that kind of logic. She had grown up with it and had it drilled into her head by her father. It wasn't true, but at one point in her life, she would have agreed with the statement. Now she knew it was part of the werewolf propaganda adopted by most werewolf hunters. It was always easier to mistreat people you didn't understand if they weren't human.

The lieutenant pushed past the sheriff to look over the ledge to the ground below. "If that's the case, then they would be in that grinder."

The sheriff looked over the ledge, his eyes drifting past Mercy, still crouched there. For a split second, she stopped breathing. She wondered if he might have seen her, but his face went red and he huffed at Lieutenant Hastings.

"Why are you telling me that instead of chasing down our quarry? Get a move on, Hastings! We'll be lucky to even get a trail with as slow as you're moving!"

"Yes, sir!" The lieutenant scrambled off. Footsteps echoed off the floorboards of her bedroom.

Mercy let out a heavy sigh of relief. She had gotten lucky, but she wasn't sure if it would happen again. She needed to make it back to the window and back inside before they spotted her up here. She tried to stand, her thighs aching for her to move, but the muscles in her back tensed all at once. Pain shot up and down her back and from side to side. She gasped in the cold air. Her back had locked up. She hissed in pain as the muscles around the middle of her back stayed tensed, locked, and throbbing. For a few seconds, all she could do was breathe, waiting for her muscles to relax. For what felt like forever, the horrible pain refused to go away.

Where had it even come from? Then she thought back to the fight she had with Rose's werewolf form in the snow, getting flung around like a rag doll outside of the shed. Then there were the tunnels used last night to escape the werewolves, crouching and crawling almost the entire time. Her back had hurt her overnight, but she had been too upset to care or notice much. Finally, she realized where it hurt the most, the spot that had locked up completely. The injury she had received falling down that hill running from Carter years ago, where a tree branch had collided with her back. At the time, it had taken days for the laceration to heal, but that was years ago. She had thought it had fully healed, but clearly it hadn't. It just had to flare up at the worst possible time.

"Mercy!" The small sharp call tore her attention away from the pain. She looked up to see Kit standing at her window, gesturing to her to come over, just as she had at the grate the night before. But her back refused to relax. Instead, it throbbed in protest.

Far below, a door slammed. It was the door that left the tower and opened up to the grinders. The two officers would be down there soon. She needed to move. She shuffled a foot forward, feeling the pain reverberate in protest.

"Come on, Mercy. I'll cover you." Kit leaned her head out of the window, her black hair flying around her face in the wind. She held a hand out and made a dramatic motion as she pointed down below to where Mercy guessed the two officers stood.

"Attack!" she hissed, her eyes wide. A shadow fell over Mercy. Then came the sound of flapping wings. A flock of crows suddenly appeared, seemingly out of nowhere. They flew down in a torrent, faster than Mercy could follow while still keeping her balance.

Dozens of them. Not as many as she had seen at Crowsmirth that day, but enough to cause some true damage. Screams and gunshots echoed up the metal walls.

A man screamed, "Run!" The cries grew more distant.

Mercy blinked. Kit had said she could control crows, but Mercy had never seen her do it before. For some reason, she had thought it was like keeping a trained parrot or maybe it was limited to the birds surrounding her old home. She hadn't expected it to be so violent or so immediate.

"Come on, come on!" Kit called. "Before they get brave and come back."

Mercy's back finally began to relax and allow her to move again, but only a little. Instead of walking, she opted to crawl to the window, not trusting her back to let her stand up straight yet. Staying on all fours actually helped her. Kit pulled her back inside, closing the window behind her.

"My back," Mercy's teeth chattered as she tried to get words out. "It locked up on me. I couldn't move."

"It's freezing out there. You're lucky you didn't freeze to death. I can't believe you went out there like that." She shook her head. "You could have fallen! I know you used to be an awesome werewolf hunter and all that, but you don't have to cheat death anymore, okay?"

Mercy held up her blankets. "It's okay, I brought a bed with me."

Kit snorted. "Where does it hurt?"

With a groan, Mercy directed her to the pain and

Kit rubbed on the tight muscles until she could stand again. Mercy hated feeling so helpless. She hated feeling so dependent on others, but she was very glad Kit was there. She was even more grateful Kit wasn't afraid to help rub out her cramped muscles.

"Come on." Kit led her out the door. "Let's get down to the lab in case they get brave and decide to do a full sweep of the place."

Kit took her hand and led her to the drainage pipe in the kitchen. Mercy sighed. She was going to have to pamper her back after she got the chance to stop and relax. She couldn't afford it locking up like this again. She hadn't really considered it a chronic injury, but perhaps it was. Perhaps she just hadn't been paying enough attention to her body these many months. Either way, she would start now. If she didn't, her back would let her know.

And she couldn't afford that happening again.

PART 2

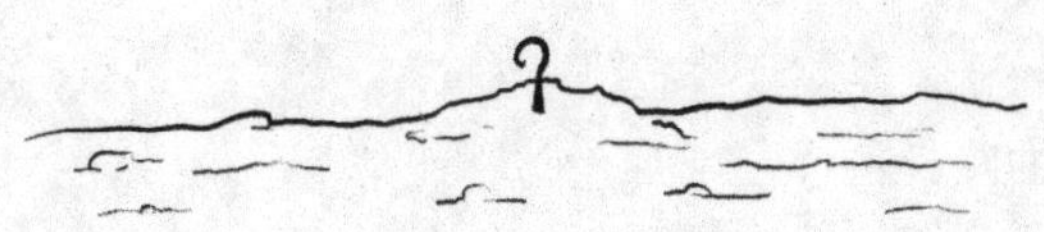

3

THE SEED OF A PLAN

THE HOT MUG of tea helped to warm her hands. The comforter from Mercy's bed was still a little damp on the outside, but the inside was still warm and dry. The blankets wrapped around her waist helped her keep warm. Her back had relaxed down to a nagging throb, which she preferred to the hot stabbing pain from earlier. Kit's quick massage had helped a lot, but she would still need to be delicate with her back for a few days until it fully healed.

The laboratory was now the only safe location in the entire Farrell Mill according to Kit. This was partly due to Mercy's brilliant idea to dismantle the front door. That meant it was easy for anyone to enter the building, from curious hunters to fully transformed werewolves. Fortunately the laboratory was sealed off by an impossibly heavy door that nobody—not even Sheriff Barlow or Lieutenant Hastings—could open. That meant they were safe there, at least for now.

A warm, furry body pressed up against her back and

Mercy had to steady herself to keep from spilling her tea. She looked gingerly over her shoulder to see Ruth curling up behind her, grabbing part of the blanket to cover her own large feet. She cocked her head to the side when she spotted Mercy watching her.

"You're fine. Take whatever you need," Mercy said, watching her loop her claws around the corner of a blanket and pull it over her body. "It does get cold down here, doesn't it?"

Ruth grunted in response.

Mercy had looked around to figure out if they could setup a coal stove or fireplace in here. Either because of Thomas' paranoia or his dedication to privacy, there were no large gaps for smoke to escape. Certainly nothing close to a fireplace. Which meant if they lit a large enough fire to stay warm, they would suffocate from the smoke.

She sighed and wished Thomas had planned his laboratory a bit better, though she knew none of them had expected this. This laboratory was probably built for him to tinker and build long before he brought werewolves down here. The space had evolved to fit his needs and then to fit Mercy's, but it wasn't meant to be a livable space.

Scuffling around the drainage tunnel told Mercy that Kit was coming back. She had gone down earlier to visit the kitchen, wanting to put together some steaming hot water skins for all of them. Kit was absolutely terrified of Mercy getting hypothermia or frostbite from standing out on the ledge hiding from the two officers. While her constant worry was endearing, Mercy worried she was pushing herself too hard. She knew how tough it was to travel through those pipes.

A pair of gloved hands appeared on the edge. Mercy put her mug aside and stood up to help. Ruth grunted over her shoulder in annoyance as Mercy headed to the pipe entrance.

"Here, give me your hand," Mercy said as she reached into the pipe.

"Thanks!" Kit was breathless, but she seemed genuinely happy about them having to hole up in the lab. Mercy helped Kit climb to her feet, noting she was definitely heavier than normal. Then she saw that Kit had strapped on several loaded satchels.

"That can't all be hot water skins," Mercy said with a laugh. "What did you find?"

Kit pulled off her gloves. "Lots of shelf-stable goods. I guess Thomas was thinking he might have to hole up at some point as well." She emptied the contents to reveal dried jerky, canned goods, and even some dried fruits. "I only took some 'cause this stuff is heavy, but also 'cause I didn't want it to look like we were living off this. If those officers come back, I don't want them to have any room to make suspicions." She gave a smirk. "We have to think ahead when it comes to that sneaky sheriff and his sidekick."

"You think they'll check the food stocks? They seemed like they were looking for intruders more than evidence of people living here," Mercy said.

"I don't think it can hurt. You said they noticed your fireplace was warm, so it makes sense that they might look for other signs of life here. I don't want them to find anything. Inside this place, we're ghosts."

Mercy blinked. That was a morbid statement.

Kit looked around. "Where's Rose?"

Mercy nodded at her office, which also used to be Thomas's personal lab space. "She's resting."

"Oh, so what you should be doing then?" Kit picked up the cans and began stacking them in the corner beside the electric prongs.

Mercy huffed. Kit was becoming an aggressive caretaker, which was both endearing and annoying. "I can't rest. Not while Andrei is stuck in a jail cell getting tortured. I don't know if I'll be able to rest again."

Kit dropped one of the cans on her haphazard pile. She turned to stare at Mercy. "Hold on, did you say tortured?"

Mercy pursed her lips. "Apparently, the sheriff tried to get information out of them this morning. I don't know what he's doing to them. They didn't go into details. I'm kind of glad because I might have been killed if I jumped through the window and attacked them." She gave a sad laugh.

Kit stared at her, slowly stacking up her cans again. "That's awful. I had no idea."

Mercy shook her head, trying to find the right words for the pain she felt. "It's bad enough that they're in jail, you know? But knowing my Andrei is getting… tortured…" Mercy couldn't finish. That tightness came to her chest and took away her breath. She pressed a hand to her chest, trying to get the pressure to go away, trying to keep herself from crying.

Kit dropped the final can onto the ground with a clatter and rushed over to her side. She put a hand on her arm. "Hey, don't get like that. Andrei is a tough guy. You saw how he transformed back at that inn in Crowsmirth. That looked super painful. And I'm sure there's nothing that the sheriff can do that could even come close to a werewolf transformation, right?"

Mercy nodded. "But if they find out what he is, they'll kill him. They won't hesitate. They'll just shoot him with a silver bullet, and that will be the end of it. They could even already know. All they have to do is press silver against his skin. What will I do if I lose him?" Mercy's heart fluttered in her chest. "I've never loved anyone like I love him. What if I never see him again to tell him?"

Kit reached down and took both of her hands, crouching down on her knees. "You're working yourself up into a state, and that doesn't help anyone. It doesn't help you, and it sure as heck doesn't help him. Okay?"

Mercy nodded, pursing her lips.

"Good. Together now. Breathe in."

Mercy sucked in a breath.

"Now breathe out."

She huffed out a shaky breath. The tension in her back and worry in her chest lessened just a little.

"Okay, now again."

They breathed together three more times, and each time they did, Mercy felt calmer and more focused than before.

"Better?" Kit finally asked, a small smile on her lips.

"Actually, I am." Mercy smiled back. "Not perfect, but definitely better."

"Good! That trick used to help me all the time when I was living in the old house with the werewolves coming to visit every night."

Mercy gave a small laugh. "You say that like they were coming for dinner."

"Oh, they definitely wanted dinner. I just wasn't on the menu."

Mercy shook her head. She still had no idea how Kit could even joke about a situation like that.

Kit stepped away. "So now that we've calmed down a bit. What's the plan?"

"I need to find out what happened with Leyda." Mercy glanced toward the office. "Preferably while Rose is asleep, so she doesn't get upset. She and Leyda were very close before everything went down."

"Yeah, she told me." Kit nodded, biting her lip. "Can we get some food prepared before we talk? I'm starving… and it's going to take some time to explain. Leyda is… how do I put this? Kind of strange."

Mercy laughed. "That's putting it mildly. Let's get some food together and pass some of the jerky out to the werewolves. Then we can figure out what we're doing next. The sooner we can get our friends out of jail, the better."

———————

EATING cold beans straight out of a can wasn't exactly Mercy's idea of a great meal, but she was too hungry after her wild adventures that morning to care. She polished off a whole can by herself and started eating from a can of peaches. Across from her, Kit was laying down on the blankets, staring up at the cavernous ceiling of the laboratory. She had her hands behind her head and was finished eating, looking like she was collecting herself. Mercy finished off her food and decided it was a good time to start talking.

"So Leyda..." Mercy started. "What happened to her? Please tell me she didn't get shot again." Mercy put her empty can on the ground, the metal ringing off of the hard floor.

Kit gave a heavy sigh and dragged a hand down her face. "I don't have all the information. I know you want everything, but I don't have it all."

"That's okay," Mercy said. "Share what you can."

Kit shuffled further into her blankets, pulling one up just below her lips. "It was late fall. We hadn't quite gotten the first snow. I was still getting settled in at the factory. Thomas had me down here cleaning cages and helping with the werewolves. I was going to start learning how to maintain the grinders soon, but I hadn't quite gotten to that point."

"Sounds like Thomas. Putting you to work right away," Mercy smirked, trying to lighten the mood at least a little.

Kit gave a small smile but didn't laugh. "It was jarring at first. I think I freaked out the first day Leyda left me here alone. For some reason, I thought the werewolves were going to break out of the cages and attack me. It doesn't make any sense, but that's what it felt like.

I couldn't stop shaking. She came back later, and I was in a corner crying." She gave a bitter laugh and wiped a tear from her cheek. "Silly me, thinking werewolves were what I had to watch out for. You would think I would know better after you got kidnapped."

Mercy winced. She wanted to say something reassuring, something that would make Kit feel better, but the words wouldn't come.

"I'm sorry." Mercy said, her voice small in the great expanse of the lab. "It wasn't your fault."

"I should have turned around. I should have looked for you." Kit squeezed her eyes shut, doing her slow breathing methods. This was not an easy story for her to tell. It was clear she was struggling to find the right words and Mercy felt guilty for wanting her to spill all the information last night. She shouldn't have pushed her. Mercy shouldn't have felt like she deserved the information without taking Kit's feelings into consideration. Mercy wasn't the only person who had been through a lot. She needed to give Kit the chance to pull herself together.

So Mercy held her tongue and waited for Kit to finish. She resisted the urge to push her or interrupt. This was Kit's story, not hers.

"The sheriff raided Farrell Mill that same day. He had his sidekick with him, along with a group of hunters. At least, I think they were hunters. They were dressed in leathers and furs, like the ones we saw in Crowsmirth. They didn't exactly identify themselves to anybody, but I could tell they were looking to hurt people."

A frown pulled at Mercy's lips. "That sounds like werewolf hunters to me."

"I don't know how they got past the guard at the front gate, but they did. They hunted down Thomas and demanded to know where the werewolves were. I guess they expected them to be attached to the grinders?"

Mercy shoved a hand into her hair. "I bet Thomas handled that well. People shoving their way into his factory and pointing guns at him."

"I was down at the base of the stairs listening to everything unfold. He said the werewolves were disposed of after he purchased them. I don't know why it even mattered, to be honest. Why did the sheriff even care as long as Thomas pays for them? This whole town is so strange!"

Mercy mulled over the scene. "Because he probably was still telling the hunters that he was going to put them to work, but he didn't. So now everybody is suspicious of the whole operation." Groaning, she dragged her hand over her face. Thomas could be so foolish sometimes. It drove her mad. "He should have known better!"

"Well, while he was talking to the sheriff and the hunters, Leyda pushed me into the lab and told me to be quiet. Then she closed the door on me! I heard all the locks go into place, and that only made me more upset. I knew better than to make noise. I was more afraid of the sheriff and his hunters than I was of the lab. At least I wasn't alone in here. The werewolves were very helpful. They saw me crying and came over to try to comfort me."

Mercy glanced at her and saw the tears streaking down her cheeks. It was in that instant she understood Thomas' plan—or at least, his plan at the time. He bought time for the vulnerable people under his care to get to safety. If any of them had discovered the werewolves kept in cages down here, they would have likely shot and killed all of them. Even Ruth and her little one. Her chest went tight at the mere thought. Leyda may have trapped Kit in here, but she also saved her from being sold off elsewhere. Perhaps the traffickers posing as werewolf hunters in Kanta had grown suspicious of the Farrell Mill workers covering their faces while they were in the streets. Perhaps they suspected the truth: that Farrell Mill was a safe house for more than just werewolves. The potential profit would have surely persuaded the sheriff to make a stand, catching everyone in the mill off guard.

"Did Leyda ever come back?"

"No." Kit wiped the tears from her cheeks and sniffled. "I heard gunshots though. Someone said a werewolf was on the loose. I don't think it was Andrei, because he had been up with Thomas at the time. I heard him talking to the sheriff at one point. But I have no idea what happened to Leyda. If she lived, surely she would have come back for me. Right? Was she the type to abandon someone like that? I didn't really know her well, but Andrei told me about her condition."

Mercy pursed her lips. In all honesty, Leyda was exactly the kind of person to abandon someone, especially if her own life and safety were in jeopardy. Or sometimes when she just felt vindictive. That knowledge wasn't going to help Kit. In fact, it would probably make her more upset.

Instead of answering directly, Mercy decided to shift focus. "Do you often have the sheriff roaming around the mill? I thought they only got in because Rose and I took down the front door last night."

"They're here all the time," Kit huffed. "They have keys to every room in the tower. I just didn't think they would be here so fast. Usually, they only check in once a week or so. It's why I stay in the pipes when I travel. It's safer that way. I guess you all have to stay down here with me for now. I was hoping you could get your room back, Mercy, since you've done so much for this place. But I shouldn't have. I almost got you captured too." She wiped away more tears, her voice breaking.

"Hey, I'm okay. It was tough there for a bit, but we made it. You can't predict what that sheriff will do. He could have just spotted the dead werewolf in the grinder and been done. You can't predict what he's going to do here or where he's going to go investigate. Don't blame yourself for any of that." Mercy shook her head, remembering back to what the sheriff said while she crouched frozen on the ledge. "I think he has a personal vendetta against this place. I'm not sure what, but he was excited about the verdict given to Thomas and Andrei. He wanted to see them suffer."

Kit turned toward her, wide eyes glinting from the fires that lined the walls.

"What verdict? What are they going to do to them?"

Mercy swallowed down the lump in her throat. Kit really didn't need to hear this right now. She wasn't in a good place, and she was clearly rattled by the officers from earlier. But she deserved to know. Kit was now as much a part of this place as Andrei. Two people she had dragged into this mess. Two people who could now be technically put on trial for helping Thomas with the mill. Two people who could now be sentenced to death because of Mercy. So many lives on the line because of her.

She took a deep breath and told Kit everything: about the verdict, about the sentencing for them to be killed in a firing squad, and about the torture. Once she started talking, it was difficult to stop. By the end of it, Kit sat across from her, shaking. No longer were her eyes full of tears. Instead, they were hard with rage. At first Mercy thought she was shaking from being so upset, but that wasn't it. Kit was furious.

"Mercy, we can't let them be killed."

She huffed in frustration. She felt inept ever since she stepped foot back in Kanta. From having to dismantle the door of the mill to having officers raid her bedroom the first night she tried to sleep. She was tired of being reactionary. She wanted to fight back. But to do that, they needed a plan.

"If only there were enough of us," Kit muttered. "Maybe we could overpower them. But there's only the two of us."

"Three, actually."

They turned to see Rose standing in the doorway to Mercy's office. She no longer looked tired or even sore. In fact, she looked stronger and healthier than Mercy had ever seen her—at her house with Oscar or at the werewolf camp.

"I heard everything about your friends." Rose strode over to the collection of food Kit had brought back. She picked up a can of salted chicken and tore the lid off with her claws before tilting it back like a drink. Mercy stared at her gaping, too stunned to speak. Kit hid a snicker behind her hand.

Rose brought the can down and gave a satisfied sigh. "I'm not letting you two head off to fight a mob of angry townspeople alone. You're taking me with you."

"But why?" Kit asked, holding a hand out to her. "No offense, but I barely know you. Why risk your life for strangers?"

Rose laughed, and Mercy couldn't help but smile at the confidence in it. "You may be more or less a stranger to me—Kit, right? But Mercy and I went through hell together. Stress like that can bond people together in a completely unique way. I trusted her with my life once, and she kept me from dying. She gave me this cure I never dreamed was possible. I owe her a life debt that I'm not sure can ever be fully repaid."

"You don't owe me anything," Mercy interrupted, recalling her own life debt to Leyda that almost turned her into a werewolf. "I don't believe in life debts." She said as both women stared at her curiously.

"Regardless, I aim to help you both." Rose smiled. "Think of it as a gift from your very enraged friend."

Mercy chuckled. "I'll take that."

Kit crossed her arms. "It's still not enough. You've seen the number of people out there. Every hunter will have a gun on them and a handful of silver bullets to go with it. We will need a bunch more people than this."

The seed of a thought began to form in Mercy's mind. A plan that just might work if they had a bunch of luck and enough time to do it. She climbed to her feet.

"Kit, you mentioned the officers who came and arrested Thomas and Andrei were wielding guns. Do you know if they had silver bullets or normal ones?"

Kit thought for a moment before replying. "I don't know. I never saw them shoot their weapons at anyone. I only heard them firing them after I got locked in here."

"By Leyda," Rose said, and Kit nodded. So she had heard everything about Leyda too. So much for trying to keep her distanced from that knowledge. Though she was a werewolf, and probably could hear them quite well even if she was resting in the next room.

"Were they firing at Leyda?" Mercy asked.

Rose clenched her jaw.

Kit blinked, "I guess so. They said a werewolf was loose."

"Was it daytime or nighttime?" Mercy asked.

"Night." Kit furrowed her brows. "Why?"

"Just… thinking," Mercy muttered to herself, staring toward the path that led out of the laboratory. She glanced at Rose. "Think you have the strength to open a very heavy metal door?"

Rose cocked her head to the side. "I would bet money you've got a plan forming. I always thought of that as your scheming face."

Mercy rolled her eyes. "I don't have a—"

"You know what?" Kit's eyes were wide. "Now that you mention it, she totally does! I don't know how I didn't notice it before."

"Look, can you open the door or not, Rose? That's all I'm asking," Mercy said.

"I can certainly try. But I'm not making any promises."

They headed through the lab, noticing several werewolves watching them as they headed toward the entrance.

"Hey, can I let the rest of them out?" Kit gestured to the cages where some of the werewolves were still fast asleep. "It's not fair for them to be cooped up when they wake up."

"Sure," Mercy said. "But be quick, we don't have much time."

Kit ran off to unbolt the cages. She had gotten quick with it like Mercy when she had been working here. Rose sidled up to her, keeping her voice low.

"About the execution. I noticed you didn't mention a date. How much time do we have to complete this plan, exactly?"

"Three days from yesterday," Mercy said. "That gives us two full days, today and tomorrow, to figure this out." She looked up into Rose's worried eyes. "Just understand. I'll do whatever it takes to keep Andrei from dying. He means the world to me and he's suffered enough. Even if my plan doesn't work out, I will do whatever it takes to keep him alive."

Rose lifted her eyebrows. "You mean even—"

"Yes." Mercy stared at her, feeling a fury and

determination she had only felt once before. That feeling had ended with Oscar on the floor, with a strike to his head from a fireplace poker. "Yes, even that."

Rose pursed her lips and nodded, her brows knotted with worry.

"All done!" Kit rushed over, breathless. She seemed excited to be doing something, anything, besides sitting here and moping about mistakes. Her energy was infectious.

"Okay, let's try this door then. I'm sure Kit will be happy not to be traveling in the drainage tunnels for a bit," Mercy said with a smirk.

"Definitely." She laughed.

Together they went up the ramp past the walls with flaming lantern oil and to the enormous metal door.

"That's a door?" Rose asked, doubt creeping into her voice. "It looks like a safe!"

"That's what I thought," Kit said.

"Keep your voices down," Mercy whispered. "We have no idea what's going on out there. The place could be swarming with officers. We have to assume the mill is occupied at all times. They could still be looking for their supposed escaped werewolf."

"Hang on, let me get something," Kit said before rushing down the ramp.

"She's a ball of energy, isn't she?" Rose chuckled.

"I think she's felt cooped up in here for so long. She's excited about any kind of plan."

Rose gave a bittersweet nod.

Kit returned a few minutes later with a strap and a

satchel on her back. "I've been waiting for when we could fight back. Here, Mercy."

She held the strap out and it took Mercy a moment to realize it was a belt with a holster and a sheath attached. It included a gun, a knife, and a couple of pouches.

"Kit, you thought of everything!" She tried on the belt and found that it fit perfectly after some adjusting. Then she opened the longer pouch and found needles with her cure. Her mouth dropped open. "But… how?"

"You left great notes for Thomas, so he was able to make a few batches for us. Figured it was a good idea, just in case."

Mercy went to her and pulled her into a hug. "Thank you. I know it's silly, but I missed having the cure on me. Even a few doses make such a big difference." She pulled away.

"You made the cure. You deserve to have it on you." Kit smiled, "You're the expert and all. If you don't get to carry it, nobody should."

"What's in the gun? Silver bullets?" Rose asked, sniffing as though the air reeked of a bad smell.

"No, regular bullets are loaded in the gun," Kit answered, sounding a little annoyed. "But if you look in the small pouch beside it, you'll find a mixture of silver and regular bullets."

Mercy opened the small pouch. She hadn't even noticed it at first. There were dozens of bullets and Mercy could easily see which ones were silver and which ones were normal. Good, she didn't want to grab the wrong ammunition. Afterward, she checked the chamber on her gun and looked at the bullets loaded there too. None of them were silver, just like Kit had said, but Mercy liked to double-check, especially when being given a gun she had never used before. She had shot her fair share of werewolves, even though she hated having to do it.

A weight lifted off of her knowing they weren't prepping to face werewolves, but people. In her experience, people were far more monstrous. She only hoped she wouldn't hesitate the next time she was in a life and death situation.

She holstered her gun and glanced at the blade. "Is that silver too?"

Kit shook her head. "No, it's just a normal blade. But it is sharp!"

"That's fine by me." Mercy glanced between them both, her body buzzing with excitement. "We ready to do this?"

"Absolutely!" Kit grinned.

Rose shook out her arms. "It all depends on if I can move this door an inch, let alone open it." She walked up to the door and put her hands on the first latch before readjusting to another latch, seeming uncertain.

Mercy walked over and put a hand on her shoulder. "You can do this," she said. "Remember the tree you moved on the road? I sure didn't help you with that."

Rose gave a quick, nervous nod.

"You're stronger now. You aren't tied to the night either. You can do more than you think."

She glanced over her shoulder, meeting Mercy's gaze. "Thank you for believing in me. I wish I believed in myself like you do." She gave a sheepish smile and turned away.

"You'll never know until you try," Mercy added.

Taking a deep breath, Rose planted her feet, gripped one of the three massive latches, and yanked. It opened. Rose gasped, taking a step back.

"Wow… I actually did it!"

Mercy smiled. "I didn't doubt you for an instant."

4

FALLING INTO PLACE

THE LARGE DOOR pulled back with a heavy thump. None of them said a word as they stared out into the empty tower. Sunlight filtered down through the metallic spiral staircase, the floating dust catching light in the air. The building felt still, as if it was holding its breath, or like a tomb. But Mercy knew better than to trust her own senses.

She turned to Rose, who was still beaming at having been able to open the door.

"Do you hear anyone?" Mercy whispered.

Rose stilled and cocked her head to the side. She sniffed at the air and Mercy remembered Andrei sniffing out werewolves in the forests of Crowsmirth the same way. Damn, she missed him.

Blinking as she pulled back from her heightened senses, Rose shook her head. "I can only smell the three of us and the werewolves in the lab. The others haven't been here for a while."

"Good," Mercy said, no longer whispering. "That

will give us some time."

"Time for what?" Kit asked. "Won't you tell us what your plan is yet?"

"Not yet." She strode into the chamber at the base of the stairs looking for something, anything, that would give her a clue her hunch was right. The black metal of Thomas' choice decor made it tough to see anything. She sighed, not wanting to give Rose dangerous hope, but she realized she needed to share her thoughts if she was going to get help.

"Look. I was thinking about what Kit said. We need numbers if we're going to save Thomas and Andrei." Her throat threatened to clench at uttering Andrei's name, but Mercy pushed through it. "She's right. But to get the numbers we need will require us to reach out to every single werewolf we have ever helped."

Kit gaped at her. "That's a lot of people! How are we going to find them all in only a few days?"

At the base of the spiral staircase, Mercy spotted a small hole. A bullet hole. She crouched down, feeling the sharp edges of the metal, and spotted the butt end of a bullet lodged inside. The shot had come from up above, one of the upper landings of the stairwell. She could tell that much from the angle, but she couldn't tell what kind of bullet it was.

"Rose, can you come and see this?" she asked.

Rose approached, followed by Kit, looking confused and a little frustrated. Mercy hoped she wasn't getting anyone's hopes up.

"It's a bullet hole," Rose whispered.

"Not just a bullet hole, but a new bullet hole. I can't

guarantee that this was a shot aimed at Leyda when she locked Kit in the lab, but it's a big clue." She stared intently at Rose. "Can you tell if it's made of silver?"

Rose blinked. "The bullet?"

Mercy nodded.

Rose clenched her jaw and got down on her hands and knees. "Move back, your silver bullets are distracting me."

Mercy did as asked.

Rose got so close to the ground, her nose almost grazed against the floor.

"Don't touch it, just in case it is silver," Kit said.

With a grunt, Rose got to her feet and wiped off her hands. "It's not silver. Just a normal bullet."

"Perfect," Mercy smiled. "Follow me, but keep checking for bullet holes. If they chased her out, maybe that will give us some idea of where she went. Maybe even where we can find her."

"You think she'll lead you to where the werewolves live. The ones who were cured?" Kit asked, her face scrunched up, wringing her hands. "She might not know anything, Mercy. She might not want to even help us. If she's even alive."

"If she is alive," Rose said with a shaky breath. "I'm going to pull her into the biggest hug I ever did. And then I'll kiss her and hold her until she finally relaxes." She shook her head. "I can't promise she'll help, but I will. I owe you both that. If we do find her..." She paused, her eyes glassy. "I don't think I'll ever be able to repay either of you." Her lips shook, and she swallowed, dropping her gaze. "I'll help to free your friends. I can't promise Leyda will want to, but I'll be there."

"Thank you," Mercy said. "You don't have to help if you don't want to either though. These are our friends and I fully understand if—"

Rose dropped a hand on Mercy's shoulder and Mercy froze in mid-sentence. "I'm going to help. Just as long as you stop second-guessing my decision to." She gave a bittersweet smile.

Mercy sighed. "That's fine." She couldn't help but give a small smile. "I appreciate it."

"I know," Rose said, a sparkle of mirth in her eyes. "Even though you have trouble believing I'll do it. I promise I'm not lying."

A weight rolled off of Mercy's shoulders at those words. She hadn't really suspected Rose was lying, had she? Even still, she struggled to understand why Rose would want to help, but she did promise. Mercy believed her.

"Thank you," Mercy said and meant it. "For understanding."

Rose gave her shoulder a squeeze before letting go.

"So these bullet holes," Kit said, wandering toward the door that led downstairs toward the bellows, "they continue this way."

Mercy pulled the door open and the chamber filled with the smell of coal and soot. The only light came from the windows up behind them. Down in the labyrinthine hallways of the bellows, there was no light, only pitch darkness.

"Thomas took me down here once. It was a maze when it was lit," Mercy muttered.

Rose came to her side. "Perfect place to hide from hunters, if you ask me. It might be dark for you, but maybe it won't be too bad for a werewolf."

"You don't think she's been hiding underneath me this entire time, do you? Crawling around these tunnels instead of coming to visit me?" Kit asked, her eyes wide. "Oh gosh, what if she's hurt and needs help?"

"Calm down," Mercy said. "We don't know anything yet. I could even be wrong about the bullet holes. They could have been there before, and I just didn't notice them. All we have right now are theories. We have to follow these clues if we want to figure this out." She eyed both of them. "Follow me. And stay close. I really don't want to lose anyone down here."

Together they descended down the steps and into the dark underbelly of Farrell Mill.

THE LAST TIME Mercy came down to these hallways, she had Thomas leading her through the cacophony of workers, and the heat from all the people employed to manage the furnaces in the bellows. At the time, Mercy had been shocked to see the number of people who worked hard beneath her feet and the enormous fires that burned bright beneath the tower. She had also felt lost once again in the belly of the mechanical mill, like she had when she was young. It was overwhelming, intimidating, and at the same time wondrous. It had shown her how much was hidden within the mill that she knew nothing about.

To see it now felt the complete opposite. The place was cold, dark, and lifeless. The monster had been slain when Thomas was arrested, leaving behind the empty. The many workers who had relied on Thomas were left without work. They hadn't treated her like the hunters of Kanta had, like easy money. She was simply a person to them. She was a nobody. It had been a relief compared to how she had been treated on the streets. She wondered what they had thought of her at the time. Maybe they expected she was Thomas' latest experiment or his latest adoption. In many ways, the mill had been an open secret in Kanta. Only a few choice people knew the full truth of what happened here. Perhaps those workers were saved by this place, like Mercy. Maybe Thomas just went from one rescue to the next, or maybe she was giving him too much credit.

"It's so dark, I can't see a thing," Kit whispered, fear lacing her words.

"It used to be bright with all the fires going down here," Kit said, making her way into the hallway. "And really hot too. I was sweating so bad when I was here last. It's strange to see it so empty and cold. It's honestly kind of sad."

"I think I can see better than you two, but I can't see well enough to spot bullet holes. Should I go make a torch or something?" Rose asked.

"I think I have an idea of where she went. Especially if she wanted to lose them down here and not get herself cornered." Mercy put her hand out on the wall, feeling for the alcoves that used to burn constantly. "Just keep close, both of you."

"Don't have to tell me twice," Kit muttered. Mercy felt Kit grab the back of her blouse. "Hold on to me, Rose. I don't want to lose you in here!"

"I'm here, don't worry. I'm hanging on."

Taking a deep breath, Mercy let her fingertips trail the wall as she walked slowly down the curving path. She closed her eyes. It was easier to remember that way. She remembered struggling to keep up when Thomas easily maneuvered the chaos of the halls. His bright red hair had been a beacon as they moved along the wall, just like this.

Her fingers trailed against the stone. It had been difficult to hear anything with the noise of the bellows down here and the constant wheeling of fuel by dozens of workers.

The stone changed to wood. A door. Mercy furrowed her brows. Had he taken the first door? She didn't recall. She felt for the cold doorknob, turned it. Locked.

"Mercy," Kit whispered, "that's not good, is it?"

"Actually, that's a good sign."

"Ugh, okay. If you say so."

Rose gave a small laugh. She was in the back of their line, which Mercy appreciated. They still had the threat of officers raiding the mill again at any time and they would be hard-pressed to make it back to the laboratory fast enough to avoid capture. At least Rose would be able to give them a heads up if anyone did follow them.

No, she didn't need to think about that. She had to focus on Thomas. Yes, he had passed by doors. Several of them, in fact.

She walked forward, more sure of herself as she pictured Thomas leading the way. He had glanced back to make sure she was still there, always looking worried, always concerned. She missed the concern in his gaze; she missed seeing his worry for her and his protectiveness. He had his flaws, but he had been good to her.

Her fingers felt wood again, but this time she let it go by, not even stopping.

"Shouldn't we try the door?" Kit asked, her voice trembling.

"Let her focus," Rose said in a warm whisper.

Yes, she needed to focus. They had passed by two doors, which meant they would get to the third one soon. Three doors, three glances back from Thomas. He had given her a reassuring smile, clearly worried she would think poorly of him. It seemed like he was always trying to get her approval, ever since she had called him out on using the werewolves as labor. Ever since, she had stood up to his bravado and grandstanding and demanded he make a change. And he had. He had changed because she asked him to. Damn, she really missed him.

Her fingers drifted over wood. She opened her eyes, but it was too dark to see anything. No wonder Kit was scared. Not that it would matter if she could see it. All the doors looked the same down here.

"Is this it?" Kit asked.

"It better be, or we're heading out of here," Rose

grumbled. So much for her saying this was a good place for a werewolf to hide. Apparently, she couldn't see that easily down here either. That supported Mercy's theory that Leyda wouldn't have stayed down here with the furnaces. She would have looked for a way to get outside.

Mercy grabbed hold of the doorknob and it turned easily in her hand. She smiled. "Found it."

She pushed the door open, and blinding sunlight spilled into the tunnel. Mercy squinted against it. Rose cried out in annoyance behind her.

"Oh, finally!" Kit cried.

Together, they stepped out onto the outcropping overlooking the dried-up riverbed and the enormous old waterwheel. On the side sat Thomas' workbench with his incomplete projects. At least the sheriff hadn't found that when the place was first emptied. Knowing that, Mercy felt a small amount of relief.

Kit stepped out toward the wheel, taking everything in. "This place is so cool! What is it?"

Mercy shut the door behind them. "It's where Thomas came to work on his many prototypes. This is where he built the Tortoise, Kit. You rode in that, remember?"

Kit blinked and turned around in confusion. "The Tortoise? Where the heck could he even fit it out here? It's way too narrow for a vehicle, let alone a beast like the Tortoise."

"Past the wheel and around the corner is where it used to sit." Mercy pointed toward the path. "Just be careful. That's a big drop down below. This place is dangerous, just like every other spot in this mill."

Kit poked her head through a pair of spokes on the waterwheel. "Wow, you weren't kidding! I could die really easy if I tried jumping here."

Mercy blinked. Kit could be so morbid sometimes.

Rose had found Thomas' workbench. He had a few unfinished wolf helmets but also, a couple he had actually finished. She held up one of the completed ones with a smirk. "Do I even want to know?"

"Yeah, I know it's weird, but we were working on a way to be anonymous so that we wouldn't be recognized later. And find a way to protect ourselves from gunshots. I came up with calling us the Wolves of Kanta. I guess the name kind of stuck."

"Gunshots?" Rose's smile faded as she held one up to inspect more closely. "I hadn't thought about how much your little miracle drug would make you targeted by these people. You would think they would be thanking you instead of locking everyone up. I never dreamed you would need to wear helmets to help people."

Mercy shrugged. "You would think, but I've learned that logic can only take you so far sometimes, especially here in Kanta. Thomas told me that because so many people rely on hunting and killing werewolves as a profession, they don't want to lose their livelihood—or their cover."

Mercy picked up one of the helmets, noting how light they were. Thomas had continued upgrading it, even when Mercy was gone. It tugged at her heart.

Rose nodded. "For selling people and claiming it's because people were victims of werewolf attacks." She put the wolf helm back on the table. "Leyda and I once thought if we lived on our own and tried to escape from normal society, we might be safe. We thought our love for each other would mean we wouldn't have to deal with hunters or traffickers ever again." She gave a heavy sigh and shook her head. "Once we were both nearly slaughtered by a small group of werewolves, we foolishly thought we could still just hide away and never be found again. I think she and I founded the first werewolf camp in Kanta—not that it did either of us any favors. It was harder to survive with more mouths to feed and more difficult to avoid hunters."

"I'm sorry you both had to be dragged into all of this," Mercy whispered. Putting the helmet back on the table, she wondered who Thomas had made that one for and if she would ever find out.

Rose gave a bitter laugh as she wiped tears from her eyes. "Just because you came up with an amazing cure doesn't mean you're responsible for lycanthropy existing, Mercy. Besides, from what Kit told me, you got dragged into this mess unwillingly as well."

Mercy gaped. "You know how I started working at the mill?"

She put a hand on Mercy's shoulder, reassuring her. "She told me everything last night after you went up to your room to bed. I'm sorry Leyda put you into that position with a life debt. That's downright mean to do to a child, even for her."

Mercy stood frozen in shock. If Kit knew all about

her background, then that meant Thomas or Andrei had filled her in too. It made her skin crawl, knowing so many people knew about her past. Not that it was exactly a secret, but she hadn't expected to be gossiped about her first night back in the mill. She didn't blame Thomas and Andrei, because they didn't know if Mercy would ever be back or if she was dead. But Kit hadn't waited even a single night to talk about her. It was kind of infuriating.

The question burning in her mind bubbled up to her lips before she could stop it. "So you know about my father. That he was a werewolf hunter."

Rose pursed her lips into a thin line and gave a short nod. "We can't all be perfect, I guess." That sparkle of mischief entered her eyes again.

Mercy gave a small huff of a laugh. "I am the very opposite of perfect. I am a jumble of emotions, and a mess of a scientist. You see the cure as amazing and I see it as a tiny stepping stone after dozens of failures. And it doesn't matter what I do. I will never fully escape my past."

"I'm sorry. I didn't mean to offend you."

Mercy shook her head. "I know, and it's not your fault. My father's shadow follows me wherever I go, and nothing I do or achieve really shakes it. He was famous in all the worst circles. And I am forever running away from those circles and coming to terms with the horrible lessons he taught me. He saw them as true, but the more I've seen, the more wrong I realize he was."

"And if he wasn't all of that, you would never have found your way here, helping us. You are needed here,

Mercy. Don't you ever forget that. I don't care how much your father's shadow creeps you out. You do good here and nothing that happened in your past will ever erase the good you do today."

A lump formed in Mercy's throat and she swallowed hard to get rid of it. "Thank you," she whispered.

Rose suddenly pulled her into a tight hug, squeezing her so hard that the breath was almost knocked out of her. Before Mercy could even speak, Rose said, "And if you hadn't found your way back here, you never would have met that cute boy I keep hearing about."

Mercy pulled away. "Andrei?" she blurted out like a child. Who else would she be talking about?

Rose nodded with a smirk. "Kit told me all about you two spending the night in that closet together."

Heat rose to Mercy's cheeks. "She did?"

"And honestly? Good for you! Take advantage of the moment, that's what I always say."

Mercy groaned, really not appreciating Kit sharing everything about her. Then again, Kit seemed super squeamish about it all at the time. She didn't even want to see Mercy and Andrei kiss. Rose must have had to pull it out of her. She was definitely more manipulative than she let on.

A loud crow's caw echoed across the outcropping, and Mercy and Rose both jumped. At the edge of the cliff, Kit stood with one boot hooked over one of the spokes of the waterwheel. A crow sat on a spoke directly in front of her face. It made small croaking sounds as it pruned its wings, fluttering them occasionally in the wind.

"That had to be uncomfortable," Kit muttered, as though speaking to a close friend. "When did that happen? Yesterday?"

More crow grumbling. It seemed to get more agitated. Or maybe that was just how crows always sounded.

"Are you sure about that location? I don't want my friends getting hurt if you're wrong."

The crow cawed loudly again and Kit covered her ears. "Ow! Okay, I get it. Sorry for doubting you."

The crow went back to its unintelligible grumbling.

Rose leaned in close to whisper into Mercy's ear. "Kit is able to speak with crows?"

"Yep," Mercy said. "And she can get them to attack people for her too."

Rose's eyes went wide.

"So probably not a good idea to get on her bad side."

"Good to know."

Kit glanced over at them and grinned. "I think my friend here has an idea where Leyda might be!"

"What?" Mercy asked, glancing at the preening crow, then back to Kit. She had seen Kit control those birds back at her bedroom, but she had never seen her talk to them before. If she had known she could talk like that with them, she might have peppered Kit with more questions, especially back in Crowsmirth.

Kit pointed into the snow-covered riverbed below. "Apparently, some mean human down there tried to throw rocks at them yesterday, and they wanted to complain to me about how violent humans can be. Honestly? Are they wrong though?"

"The bird told you this?" Rose was clearly struggling to get past the talking bird part.

"Sure!" Kit hopped down off the waterwheel. "The crows here in Kanta are still getting used to having a human around who can talk with them, but word gets around fast with crows." She put a hand out to ruffle the crow's feathers around its neck and head. "Pretty soon I'll have a bunch of crows as my friends here too, just like I did in Crowsmirth. It just takes time and trust."

Something clicked in Mercy's mind, like a puzzle piece falling into place. "And how many friends do you think you've made in Kanta so far, Kit?"

"Bird friends?" she asked.

Mercy nodded.

Kit thought for a moment. "I would guess about ten or so. Well, eleven now it seems, not including all the crow family and crow friends. I haven't met all of them yet."

Mercy walked up slowly, wondering if she might get to pet the crow too, but as she got close, the bird hopped farther down the spoke.

"They're not really in a friendly mood today," Kit said. "Don't take it personally."

Mercy stared at the crow's shiny black eyes. "Do you think your friends would help us with our plans if you asked them?"

"Maybe. Depends on how dangerous it is. The momma crows really don't like their babies getting hurt."

Mercy watched the bird hop down from the water-wheel and take off over the snowy riverbed. The seeds of a plan took form. More pieces fell into place and her hope increased. It wasn't much, but it was a beginning. Of course, Mercy knew she would have to find Leyda for it to fully sprout.

"Kit, can you take us to where the crows saw the human?"

Kit grinned. "It's down there, so it's going to be a cold walk. But I can show you where they said they were attacked."

"And if Leyda isn't there?" Rose asked, farther back from the edge and looking reluctant to get too close.

"We have to try. We don't have a choice." Mercy glanced up to the sun to see it was beyond its apex in the sky. "And we're running out of daylight."

PART 3

5

SEND A MESSAGE

ROSE OFFERED to go back to the tower and fetch coats and hats for the trek down into the snowy riverbed. The only requirement she had was the door to the outcropping be kept open, so she could see her way back. Mercy stood with her back against the door waiting for Rose, her mind ever turning.

If Leyda was down there, why hadn't she gone back to the mill? Why had she stayed down there throwing rocks at birds? If it wasn't Leyda, what then? Mercy knew they needed numbers to break Thomas and Andrei out of jail. There weren't enough of them on their own, and crows couldn't make up for their few numbers. They needed people who wanted to help Andrei and Thomas.

Mercy didn't want to just break her friends out of jail either. The more she thought about it, the more she wanted to do, the more she wanted to fight back. She wanted to send a message. One that would be heard across the land, whispered about between werewolf hunters and warned about by corrupt officers in other towns. Even if they did break them out, right now she had no assurance they would be safe and left alone. She wanted assurance, not a temporary resolution. She wanted to feel safe again, to know security. She was tired of running and tired of dealing with these people.

Leyda was the key to all of it. If they could only find her.

"Mercy, you okay?"

Mercy looked up to see Rose taking long strides across the darkened hall toward her. She carried a large bundle of fabric: a combination of coats, hats, and gloves.

"Sorry, just thinking." She took her items, careful not to let Rose drop the others.

"It does no good dwelling on it all. Just focus on each step forward. One step at a time. Otherwise, you'll stress yourself out before we're even on the ground."

Mercy nodded and pulled the door closed behind Rose as she stepped outside. She appreciated Rose's concern, but plotting how to help her loved ones actually made her calmer, more focused. It helped her see the bigger picture, to put things into perspective, but it wasn't worth explaining. Rose would say she was over-analyzing everything, which might be true, but considering the short time limit they had, to Mercy it seemed logical.

"Did you run into any trouble?" Mercy asked, avoiding the comment.

"No trouble, but I made sure to bolt the lab closed just in case. I didn't want anyone to go snooping inside."

She pulled on her own coat with Mercy's help. "I'm sure those werewolves can take care of themselves, but we don't need to give the sheriff any more reason to search this place."

"Oh, good." Kit came around the corner at the far end of the outcropping. She grabbed her coat and pulled it on in a hurry. "It's windy out there. The covering here really helps keep the wind out. You can't tell, but this place is really protected."

Mercy arched an eyebrow at her. "Where have you been? Finding more bird friends?"

Kit pulled a fuzzy hat down over her ears and pulling on a pair of gloves. "I looked, but I couldn't find any. I think it might be too cold for them to come out much right now. I did find tire tracks though. You said that place around the corner is where the Tortoise is usually parked?"

"Usually parked? It's not there?" Mercy felt a pit of worry drop into her stomach. "Surely the sheriff didn't confiscate it. I didn't think they knew about this back area at all."

"I don't think so," she said with a worried expression. "The tracks lead down into the riverbed."

Mercy let out a slow breath, trying to figure out what that meant. Had someone stolen the Tortoise and taken off with it? As big as that vehicle was, it would be difficult to hide.

She pulled on her own knitted hat, careful to cover her ears. "Show me."

THEY WALKED CAUTIOUSLY around the thin ledge that connected the outcropping to the road where the Tortoise had always rested. It was more treacherous than Mercy remembered, or maybe she had just been rattled by her own near-death experience on the ledge outside of her bedroom earlier.

Kit climbed across with ease and trotted toward the far end of the path, kicking up snow, dirt, and gravel in her wake.

Mercy shivered. Kit was right. It was freezing as she stepped away from the outcropping and out onto the thin path. Icy wind whipped past her face and she gasped at the intensity. Her nose felt the worst of it, but even her eyes were chilled, and she blinked as cold tears formed. She was grateful to Rose for grabbing coats, gloves, and hats. If she hadn't, Mercy would be freezing her butt off even more. She pulled her gloves down tighter under her coat sleeves and pulled her hat down farther, shielding more of her face.

The wind howled around her and Rose as they made their way across. It sounded so similar to the werewolf howls she had heard back at her home that it gave her chills. Werewolf howls were distinct with unique tones, not unlike wolf howls. She had heard them on the wind so many times, the sounds distorted over distances, and they still made her anxious. She had gotten used to Silver and Jamison's howls, but the howling wind sounded just similar enough to a werewolf's howl, and just wrong enough, that it made her skin crawl.

Kit called back to them, but her voice was carried away by the wind.

"Did you get that?" Mercy asked.

"Not a single word, and I'm a werewolf," Rose sighed.

They took their time catching up with Kit, who stopped near to some large tire tracks.

"See? They go off the ledge here and down the ramp. You don't think the sheriff crashed it, do you?"

Mercy crouched down, tracing her fingertips along the deep grooves the tire tracks had made. They weren't recent. The snowfall had partially filled in the tracks. She could feel the powdery layer on top and the icy layer beneath it before she hit the dirt and gravel. Could these have been made months ago? She couldn't be certain. She had been taught how to track werewolves in the forest, not vehicles on high, windy cliffs.

Kit's boots crunched on gravel and ice as she pointed over her shoulder down the main road. "This road leads to Main Street, right? But I couldn't find tracks that went that way. At least, nothing fresh."

"Relax a little, please?" Rose asked. "Let Mercy focus. I'm curious about these tracks first, before we look at anything else."

Mercy climbed to her feet. "I think these tracks are old. Possibly weeks, maybe even months old. Or the ground is just softer here, but with all the gravel, I don't think so." She stared for a long moment before shaking her head. "I'm sorry. Tracking this thing is hard. I was trained to be a werewolf hunter. This is very different."

Kit came over, glanced to the tracks at Mercy's feet and back over the ledge. "So which way? Do you still want to head down into the riverbed and trust my crow and these tracks, or do you want to see if there are any tracks heading to Main Street?"

With a sigh, Mercy dragged a hand over her face. "Honestly? I trust your crow over my vehicle-tracking skills any day. This is not my strength."

Rose laughed.

"That's fine. We can always check the other road if we have to. Can I take point?" Kit asked, already heading down the slope toward the riverbed below.

"Looks like you already are!" Rose chuckled, her breath coming out in short, cloudy puffs.

"Just be careful," Mercy warned. "We still don't know who is living down there. Yes, it could be Leyda, but it might be someone else. Someone wanting to take advantage of the chaos at the mill and steal the Tortoise. It could be anyone. Maybe an individual, or a whole werewolf pack for all we know."

Kit froze in place, scanning the vast white blanket of snow that covered the old riverbed. "Um, in that case, I don't know if I want to take point any longer."

Mercy caught up with her, shoving her hands into her pockets to try to keep them warm. "That's fine. Just direct me where to go." She looked closer at Kit and realized the younger girl was shaking. "Are you okay?"

Kit gave a short nod, breathing fast, her arms splayed out to her sides like she was frozen to the spot. "Yeah, I just… I hadn't thought about the werewolf pack. I should have, I know. But I didn't."

Mercy put a hand on her shoulder. "Don't worry. It's daytime, remember? If we do run into a werewolf pack, they'll all be in human form, not werewolf form."

She bit her lip and gave another quick nod. "I know. I just..."

Mercy waited for her to gather her thoughts.

"I haven't forgotten about Crowsmirth, or my old home, you know? The werewolves in the lab are fine. They're sweet and usually well-tempered. I've gotten used to them. They've been really kind to me. But... I don't want to go against a transformed werewolf pack. Not again. I don't know if I can handle it."

Mercy took her hand and gave it a squeeze. Kit's hand shook in hers. "I don't blame you. And if that happens, you go back to the mill and take the tunnels to return to the laboratory. Okay? You don't have any need to stay out here and try to handle anything. You go back and get safe."

Kit gave another jerky nod.

"Nobody will be upset. This kind of work isn't for everybody. Nobody will blame you."

"I know," she cried, her face scrunching up. "But you all need me and I want to help!"

"We need your help, but I don't want you to freeze up. If you freeze up, you can get hurt. Fear can make people not think straight, and that's when it's dangerous. I had that problem myself when I first tried to capture a werewolf."

"Really?" Kit blinked. "You're always so brave and confident. I can't even imagine you freezing up, Mercy. Was it... scary?"

"Yeah, it was terrifying." Mercy breathed in the cold air. "I was taught to be bait, to lead the werewolf into a trap and then hit the trigger. Then run for it before the cage fell. I practiced the move over and over again. I thought I had perfected it, but I was too slow. I saw the werewolf's eyes and… I froze up and couldn't move."

Kit stared at her with a look of horror on her face.

"It took me years of training to get to that point. Years of practice, and I still got scared. You don't know how you're going to react until you're in the middle of it. I don't want that to happen to you."

Kit pursed her lips and looked down.

"Remember," Mercy said. "If you need to run, do it. I would rather you be safe and embarrassed than brave and dead."

Biting her lip, Kit finally looked up again and met Mercy's gaze. "Thank you. I was afraid that I wouldn't know what to do. That I would get scared and you all would get hurt because of me."

Mercy pulled away. "No problem. If you need my permission to run for safety, you have it. You're one of the few friends I have left. I just want you safe."

Kit wiped at her eyes with a weak laugh. "Stop already! You're going to make me cry and it's too cold out here to cry."

Mercy snickered. "Sorry."

"Come on," Rose said, coming up behind them. "Let's get down there before we lose all the daylight and Kit starts bawling her eyes out."

Mercy took the lead, shaking her head.

"It's not my fault. Mercy started hitting me with emotions! I'm not used to having human friends, let alone friends who tell me they're worried about me." She sniffled.

Mercy smiled as they made their way down the slope, and onto the snow-covered riverbed. She hoped her advice helped. She remembered just how close she had come to death that night with her father, and she never wanted to see Kit put into a situation like that. It hurt even more knowing her father had been risking her life for absolutely no good reason. It had all been propaganda, all lies.

If it helped Kit not be afraid to run away if she had to, at least it helped somebody.

THE BENEFIT of going down into the riverbed was that the wind wasn't so bad. Something about the corners and bends on Farrell Mill made it very windy when there was any wind at all. The downfall was all the ice they had to walk over to get anywhere.

Mercy should have expected the ice to be bad when she noticed the thin layer at the bottom of the tire tracks up on the outcropping. Even though the riverbed had been drained, it still gathered water after any rain. The still water turned into slushy, slippery ice in these temperatures. The riverbed had effectively turned into a giant drainage ditch and the soft, powdery snow on top hid the dangerous ice.

The slope down to the bottom was more treacherous than expected and the hidden ice meant they fell or at least lost their balance frequently. Mercy had the worst time with it, pinwheeling her arms each time before catching herself on her palms as she fell. Kit didn't struggle as bad as Mercy, but when she did fall, she often landed flat on her butt. Rose didn't fall once, but she had a few choice words for the snow, the ice, and the freezing temperature.

By the time they made it to the bottom, they were all bruised and sore, and slightly more annoyed at having to go down there than they had been at the top.

"I sure wish my crow friends weren't so small. If they could have flown me down here, I would have done anything they asked. I would have given them as many shinies as I could find."

"Did you ask them?" Rose asked, still managing a smile and a bit of mirth despite it all.

"No, that would have been rude!" Kit huffed a cloud of breath into the crisp air. "I'm trying to make friends, not chase them away."

Mercy looked out over the expanse of the riverbed. It was difficult to tell from up on the overhang, but here on the ground level, she could see just how massive the river had once been. Down here, she spotted the occasional signs of its old life that she had missed from above.

Poking out from the snow-covered tall grass was a ship's wheel, complete with hand carved decoration along the wood. Probably some sunken ferry boat carelessly cleaned up after the dam was built and the river diverted. Off to the side, she spotted half of the hull of a small boat partially buried in the dirt. It could have once been a shipping boat.

Walking across the flat field, her boots crunching on the layers of ice and snow, Mercy saw how Kanta used to be. Not the small, superstitious town crowded with werewolf hunters and human traffickers eager to make a quick buck, but a bustling trade town. A mill with a giant waterwheel. A thriving fishing community.

The wind swept around her face, making her nose run and her eyes cold. For a brief quiet moment though, she saw what life could be like if her cure was fully embraced. She glimpsed the bustling, thriving world her mother and father had called home. She imagined them going down to the pub in the evening, talking with fishermen and ship captains. How she wished she could have seen the world like they had. Her heart ached for a world she would never know.

A thousand possibilities of what lives she could have lived sprawled out before her, like a roll of parchment, listing off all the unrealized potentials. She could have helped her mom at the pub, learn to be a fur trapper with her father, maybe even learned to sail a ship and go up and down the river with her wares.

Before the werewolves. Before her mother's death. Before the world had completely crumbled to the forsaken ruins she now called home. Was it possible her cure could return the world to its former normalcy? To live through nights without constant fear of werewolf attacks, to not have to limit travel to only daylight hours, and maybe even to walk the streets of any town without fear of showing who she was, or fear of capture. That was what Mercy wanted, what she could see in those faint skeletal remains that dotted the landscape.

Was she asking for too much? Was normal an impossible feat? If she could find a way to get her cure accepted, appreciated, and distributed, maybe some form of that normalcy wasn't so far off. Maybe in some meager form, it had a chance to become a reality. Maybe, if she worked hard enough, she could glimpse at least a version of that world her parents had taken for granted.

"Mercy?"

She turned to see Kit staring at her with sympathy. "It's a lot to take in, isn't it?"

"It is," she said, looking around at the barren waste-land around them. "Do you think Kanta will ever be normal again? I mean, do you think all this will ever come back? The ships, the trading, the bustle that used to be normal here?" She gestured helplessly to the pieces of life poking out of the earth like discarded headstones.

"I mean, I guess we might see ships if those rich people up north ever decide to take down their dam, but the rest of it?" Kit shook her head. "No, I think Kanta is too messed up for that. Crowsmirth too. And honestly, maybe that's a good thing?"

"Good?" Mercy asked, allowing Kit to turn her around and lead her back toward the side of the riverbed where Rose waited for them. "Look at how we live here. We're always hiding, having to disguise ourselves. We can't live out in the open doing whatever we want. We have to hide in the shadows. How can that be good? Why shouldn't we want what our parents had?"

Kit turned to her with a heavy sigh. "Because our Kanta today came from those people. They're the ones who thought that paying for werewolf heads was a smart way to deal with the problem."

"You're talking about the lords up north?"

Kit nodded. "That old Kanta made it so three women like us can't walk on the street without hiding who we are. Old Kanta decided to take advantage of a werewolf outbreak and start capturing women to sell for any reason. They're the ones who stole me and my mom. I hope we never go back to that world. If that's what's considered normal, I hope Kanta gets weird and strange, and embraces a new direction. They tried that path out once and it did not work in the long term. Werewolves came along, and those greedy jerks were quick to change hunting animals for hunting people. That's the kind of people it created. I think it's time for something better. Like your cure! Let's bring good things into the world for once instead of all the bad things they brought."

Mercy hadn't thought of it like that. Kit was right though. The Kanta her parents came from had good people, but also too many of the greedy jerks Kit mentioned were quick to use others to make a quick buck. It had led to the werewolf outbreak going unchecked, to women being traded, to people like Thomas using werewolves as labor. That was what came of the world where her parents grew up. A world that was unprepared for werewolves, let alone anything else.

Mercy wrapped an arm around her shoulders. "Thank you. For talking sense into me."

"No problem," she muttered. "I told you, I want to

help. And if that means knocking sense into you now and then, I'm all for it!"

They got back to the wall to see Rose sniffing at the air. Only she kept getting interrupted because she kept sneezing.

"Anything?" Mercy asked after her sneezing fit had passed.

"I can't smell anything useful." She sniffed. "And every time I think I've gotten something, I start sneezing again and lose it." She grumbled in frustration.

"It's probably the cold," Mercy muttered as a chill went up her spine. "The wind is really strong against the wall here too. It's probably working against us." She turned to Kit. "Is this where your crow said they saw someone?"

Kit looked around, then up above their heads. Mercy followed her gaze and looked up to see they were directly beneath the giant wooden waterwheel. She hadn't noticed that before. Standing beneath it, she realized just how massive and heavy the waterwheel was. No wonder Thomas never had it dismantled or moved. She suddenly felt very uncomfortable to be standing beneath it.

"No…" Kit said after a moment. "It's farther along the wall. This way." She led the way as they went around the rounded wall of the riverbed. The tall towers of Farrell Mill loomed over them. At this angle, the mill looked even more like a monster or a sentry.

After walking awhile, Mercy realized she couldn't see the tall tower of the mill at all. Only a couple of spokes from the waterwheel were still visible. For some reason, she hadn't realized there was a place down on the riverbed that wouldn't be visible from the tower. It was unsettling. Someone could hide out here without being seen by anyone in the tower, or even anyone from Kanta either.

This would be the perfect place for a group to hide out without being seen by anyone. A hiding place in plain sight. Surely the sheriff or any of his officers wouldn't come down here either. They would see this as a wasteland. Who could possibly survive down here in the cold wind and ice? Unless the people were very scrappy and willing to eat anything at all. A chill went down her spine.

"Hey, Kit!" Mercy cried out, but it was too late. Mercy had been so focused on the towers and the water-wheel above their heads she hadn't noticed Kit was so far ahead. Judging by the way she was strolling, Kit hadn't realized it either. Mercy had called out to her, but she hadn't heard. Just like up above on the outcropping.

"What's the problem?" Rose asked, but there wasn't time to explain.

Mercy sprinted forward, cupping her hands over her mouth. "Kit!"

Finally Kit stopped and turned around. Confusion echoed in her stance. Mercy made dramatic gestures for her to come back, regroup, so they could move in as a team. Kit took a step or two toward them, clearly confused and concerned.

Something fast darted out toward her from the wall. Kit screamed. Mercy ran as fast as she could to catch up.

6

SECRETS

MERCY DIDN'T THINK she only ran. She screamed as she pumped her legs, slipping only occasionally on the icy ground. The shadow that had darted out from the wall leaped away again, but Kit was on the ground.

Catching up with her, Mercy crouched down beside her. Kit sat on the ice, breathing hard and eyes wide. She didn't look like she was hurt. Mostly she looked shocked.

"What happened?" Mercy asked, trying to catch her breath.

Kit stuttered, shook her head, then looked past her, behind her. "Mercy!"

Before she could react, a warm hand wrapped around Mercy's throat and cold, sharp metal was placed against her throat. A knife.

"We don't mean any harm!" Mercy said in a terrified voice. "We're just looking for a friend. Please don't hurt me!"

She heard a gasp and the knife was pulled away.

Rough hands turned her around in the snow—too strong to fight, too strong to be merely human. Caramel eyes met hers. For the first time all day, Mercy breathed a sigh of relief.

"Leyda!"

She was dressed in thick cloaks, but all of them had holes. Her face was wrapped in thick strips of fabric that had clearly been worn again and again. She had even used scarves beneath the strips of fabric to give them some stability. Her eyes were rimmed with red as she glanced between Kit and Mercy, confusion plain on her face.

"It's us. It's Mercy, remember?" Mercy asked.

"Mercy?" The word was more of an animal's grunt than a word.

Suddenly Mercy understood why Leyda hadn't returned to the tower. Those were gunshots in her robes and, judging by the difficulty she had even saying her name, she hadn't spoken to anyone in a very long time. Possibly in all the months since she had come out here. That wasn't a good sign at all.

Mercy slowly moved her hands down to take one of Leyda's, the one not holding a rusty knife. "Do you remember me?" Leyda's mechanical arm felt unnaturally warm in her hand, too warm for the chill of the snow and wind.

Leyda nodded as tears filled her eyes. It hurt Mercy to see her clearly struggling to speak another word. It was so unlike her that it was heartbreaking.

Mercy looked to Kit slowly getting to her feet. "And Kit? You remember her, right?"

Leyda had to stare at her for a moment too long before giving a slow, uncertain nod.

"It's okay," Kit said with a nervous wave. "I'm not very memorable."

"Leyda?" Rose asked. She had stood not far off behind Leyda, watching, taking everything in. Mercy wondered if she was having trouble recognizing the love of her life like this. Mercy wasn't sure if she would have known her, if it hadn't been for her mechanical hands shifting her around, or being so close to see her eyes.

For a moment, Leyda didn't move. She just stood there like a statue and Mercy wasn't sure if she had heard any of them. Then Leyda swallowed hard and turned around to face Rose, still loosely holding onto Mercy's hand.

"Rose?"

To Mercy's untrained ear, it sounded more like a bark than a name. But Rose nodded and held out her arms as tears spring to her eyes. "I've missed you so much, my love!"

Leyda dropped Mercy's hand and the rusty knife, and ran to Rose, pulling her into a hard embrace. Rose let out a gasp as Leyda clung tightly to her.

"Is she okay?" Kit asked, standing at Mercy's elbow. Fear pricked at her voice. "I don't remember her being so…"

"Animalistic," Mercy said, pursing her lips with worry.

Kit nodded.

Mercy had to agree with her. What had happened to Leyda? As far as Mercy knew, she had been just fine when she locked Kit in the laboratory and ran for cover. But something must have happened. Something must have prevented her from going back to the mill to see Kit. Judging by her trouble speaking, it had to be something bad.

Along the wall was an enclave Leyda must have used as shelter. It wasn't much, but it would be protection from the snow and the rain. It reminded Mercy of the werewolf camp with a smoldering campfire for cooking and warmth, and piles of discarded refuse stuffed into the corners—rags, skeletal remains of animals, and a few used up satchels. Mercy got closer. Leyda had been living here for a while. She picked up one of the empty satchels. Out fell a few crumbs of trail mix.

Behind her, Rose was trying to calm Leyda, who was crying. No, she was bawling her eyes out. Mercy turned to see Rose rocking Leyda in her arms. They sat on the ground together, Leyda draped over Rose, tears streaming down her cheeks. All of that anger she had seen pinned up in Leyda for so many years was now pouring out. All that pain and longing had been distilled into a single, long and wailing cry. Rose had the cure. She was, for the most part, human. Leyda was still stuck in her partial transformation. She was still stuck in that personal hell. Something horrible had happened to Leyda, something bad enough to break her to the point of losing the ability to talk. It was all so heartbreaking.

Kit gripped her arms as she trailed behind Mercy, looking afraid and lost. Mercy urged her closer and put the empty satchel into Kit's hands, keeping her voice low.

"Do you recognize this at all?"

Kit took it, dusting off the powdery snow and turning it over in her hands.

"I haven't seen this since… the Tortoise."

"That's what I thought too. Thomas used to keep it stocked in there. But I don't see it anywhere, do you?"

They turned in the small enclave that only provided a partial shelter from the elements. It was difficult to believe Leyda had called this hovel a home for so many months. Or that she would choose this place over the mill if she had access to the Tortoise. What in the world had happened? This place wasn't up to Leyda's usual standards. It almost looked like she hadn't figured out how to get back. But that didn't make any sense.

"There!" Kit cried, rushing to the back of the enclave to a giant boulder. She squatted down and dug out a pile of animal skeletons and rags to get to a small gap at the bottom.

"Kit, what is it?"

She gestured for Mercy to join her. When she did, she helped clear out the small items of debris from the corner. Once cleared out, Mercy could see behind the boulder and into the shadowy depths it had hidden. It took a moment for Mercy's eyes to adjust to the darkness inside, but then she spotted it: the back tire of the Tortoise.

This wasn't an enclave at all. It was the entrance to a cave Leyda had closed off with the Tortoise hidden inside.

"But why?" Mercy asked. "Why did she bury it back there?"

"I have no idea," Kit said. "But she's the only one who could get it out."

IT TOOK some work to convince Leyda to open up the cave so they could retrieve the Tortoise. For some reason she was very reluctant to pull back the boulder. The more she resisted, the more Mercy worried what they would find. She had never known Leyda to be so animated or so resistant. She didn't want to talk about the boulder, didn't want to talk about the Tortoise. It was all bizarre, and it made Mercy anxious. Watching her wring her hands as she paced back and forth again and again around the cave entrance made the hairs stand up on the back of Mercy's neck.

It was dusk by the time Leyda finally agreed. Together with Rose, Leyda pulled the boulder back inch by inch until the Tortoise was finally revealed and the boulder shoved out beside the cave entrance. It was twilight by the time Mercy got a good look at the space where the Tortoise was hidden.

Covered in cobwebs and sunk slightly in the dirt, the Tortoise had certainly seen better days. Mercy hoped it would still drive. They would need it. If it didn't, they had no experts at hand to help. Both Thomas and Andrei were in jail and she wouldn't even know what tools to bring down from the mill to try to fix it.

Kit hurried ahead, excitement brimming in each step. But a bad feeling made Mercy's stomach clench. She couldn't put words to it. If she was asked, she wouldn't be able to explain it. It was just a bad feeling that gnawed at her insides, like her panicky feeling that had made her grab her clothes and go out on the ledge of her bedroom. Something was very wrong. It was similar to the feeling she'd had when she found the werewolf cage out in the middle of the woods from her father's truck. A sinking feeling that made her tremble from head to toe.

"Kit, stop!" she cried, not wanting something bad to happen to her friend. Not Kit, who was terrified of werewolves. Not the girl who had already survived so much and been through too much. Mercy was afraid of something she couldn't put a name to.

Kit came to an immediate stop and turned around with wide eyes. "Mercy?" she asked. "What's wrong?"

She didn't know what to say. Something about the Tortoise being buried back there spoke of embarrass-ment, not safety. Something in how Leyda paced but never met her eyes. Something that made her think of Oscar's beat up truck hidden like a secret inside of the shed. Something bad had happened in there. Something she definitely didn't want Kit to see.

She stepped forward and put a hand on Kit's shoul-der. It was meant to be reassuring, but Mercy's hands were shaking.

"Let me take a look first." She hoped she sounded calm and collected, even though she felt neither.

Kit didn't argue or ask more questions, which Mercy appreciated, and took a few steps back. Kit trusted Mercy's instincts, and she appreciated that.

It was a tight squeeze between the Tortoise's doors

and the wall, but Mercy could fit. It was darker than she liked with the sun close to setting outside. She reached for the front door handle and something crusty scraped against her gloved hand. She pulled her hand back to hold up to the dwindling sunlight. Something dry and coppery powdered against her hand.

Mercy had seen that shade before in the werewolf cages she had to clean out from her father. She had seen it in places around Farrell Mill and had worked closely with it when crafting her compounds.

It was blood.

She brought it to her nose and smelled a vague, sulfuric scent. The anxiety that rattled her entire body released just a little. It was werewolf blood and not human. That made her feel a little better.

Leyda still paced at the entrance, her feet moving faster over the snowy ground. What was she so anxious about? What was she reluctant to show them?

Heart thudding fast in her chest, Mercy pulled open the front door. What she saw made her entire body grow cold.

The entire front two seats of the Tortoise were covered in blood. It was so thick the fabric beneath couldn't be seen. It didn't stop on the seats either. The blood carried up along the ceiling in a splatter formation. The longer she stared at it, the more she could see. She didn't want to see it. She didn't want to be here. She wanted to run.

It wasn't just blood; she realized as her stomach dropped. She could see pieces of something scattered across the fabric. It took Mercy too long to identify what it was.

She only barely registered dropping away from the door, stumbling out of the cave, tripping and nearly falling to the ground. She remembered seeing Kit's confused, questioning gaze. The blast of cold air on her face helped. She took in heavy breaths, feeling her insides quake. The cold helped sate her frazzled nerves. It helped to ease the complete assault her senses had taken.

A gloved hand took hers and she realized Kit had moved beside her. Fear and concern battled in her eyes.

"What happened?" she asked in a small voice. "What did you see? Was it bad?"

Mercy stared at her as her body slowly relaxed, slowly getting back to normal.

Kit squeezed her hand. "It's okay, you can tell me."

Mercy didn't intend to be blunt. She planned to soften the blow, ease the information dump. But after all the research she had done, her mind didn't like to do that. Especially when she was scared or upset. It tended to shift into cold, hard facts and clinical analysis when it was difficult to speak her mind in any other format. So she said the first thing that came to mind, as cruel and blunt as it was.

With a heavy sigh, Mercy allowed the bite of the air to fill her lungs before letting it all out.

"Leyda—" she said with a voice filled with far more steel than she felt. "Someone blew her brains out in the front seat."

IT WAS FULLY dark by the time they made it back to the overhang that led into the mill. They shuffled without a word into the darkened hallway, following Rose. Careful to check for any sign of movement beforehand, they slipped through the empty tower. A crescent moon sent limited light down to them through the metallic spiral staircase. Working together, Rose and Leyda quickly opened the door to the lab. Mercy caught the first whiff of lantern oil from the wells along the walls and relief washed over her.

For all its faults, the lab was her safety, her oasis amid the terror and confusion of the outside world. The lab was a retreat where science and logic reigned supreme and there was a strange comfort in that. Here, Mercy felt in charge. Here, she felt like she had power over something, even if it was a small place compared to the rest of the world.

"Kit." Mercy pulled her aside after the others had already gone down the ramp. "I need you to go to the kitchen and get as much food as you can carry. Jerky is preferable if you can find it, but it's not absolutely necessary. Get what you can. Leyda is going to need all she can get to fully recover in time."

Kit blinked at her. "Recover? But I thought she got shot months ago."

Mercy nodded. "She did. And she never fully recovered, Kit. That's the problem. That's why she never went back to the mill and why she struggled to recognize us. I don't think she's been eating well. And that means her recovery is slow—if it happens at all. We've got to help her."

"My crow friend!" Kit cried. "That's why she was throwing rocks at them. I bet she was trying to knock them out of the sky to get food." Her gaze darkened at the thought.

Mercy nodded. "That's what I think. But we need her now more than ever. I need what she knows and to get that, we will need her to fully recover. I need her to be able to talk with me. So we need to try to speed her recovery as much as possible."

Kit furrowed her brows. "Please tell me it's also because you're worried about her and want her to get better. It isn't only about the information, is it?"

Mercy blinked at her. "Of course not! I just want to help Thomas and Andrei get out of jail." That familiar tightness came to her chest at Andrei's name. "I just want everyone to be alive. I want all of us to be safe. To do that, I need Leyda to talk to me."

Still, Kit stared at her with concern. "And what happens if we can't? What if, despite everything, somebody gets killed? What if Leyda doesn't want to talk? You can't rely on her to do this, Mercy. She's been through a lot."

Mercy gaped at her. She had never heard Kit talk like this, especially not to her. Then again, Mercy knew her own weaknesses. She knew she could sometimes get cold when it came to her work, when she got too focused. Sometimes, admittedly, when it came to Leyda too. Andrei had pointed it out to her before. She had a bad habit of always seeing the worst in Leyda but in her defense, Leyda had been often mean or cruel to her. So, instead of the retort that wanted to spring to her lips, she pursed her lips closed and gave a more thoughtful answer instead.

"If someone does die, then at least I'll know I did as much as I could. I'll know that I tried my best." The very thought of Andrei getting killed threatened to send her into a shaky, crying mess. So she focused on Thomas instead. It helped at least a little.

"You mean *we* tried our best?" Kit reached out to squeeze her forearm. "Cause we're all in this together, right? We're working as a team, Mercy."

Mercy swallowed hard and gave a short nod.

"Good. Cause we're working hard too."

Mercy whispered. "Okay. Thank you for keeping my head straight."

"That's what friends are for." Kit turned and headed up to the kitchen, leaving Mercy alone with her thoughts.

Kit was a good person, probably a better person than Mercy was in a lot of ways. She understood Kit was trying to help her, trying to get her to share the weight of everything. But Mercy knew she was the one who would lose the most if Thomas and Andrei were killed. She would be lost, back to square one. She would return to being that scared little girl who was rescued in the woods. She couldn't go back to that. She couldn't allow herself to be that fragile again. She had barely survived it then. Back when she was living in Oscar's house of horrors, trying to survive and escape each and every day, the only thing that had kept her going was Andrei's love. She understood Kit was trying to get her to share, but Mercy knew she would fall apart without Andrei. It was a truth she had been slowly realizing ever since she found out he was in jail.

How could Mercy possibly survive if she didn't have anyone to survive for? Yes, there was Kit, who had become a best friend. And Rose, who Mercy had been bound together with under Oscar's tyranny. Leyda had always hated her, always barely put up with her. It wouldn't be the same. She wouldn't be the same. After all she had been through, she was tired of having those she loved wrenched away from her. She was tired of losing her freedom, her friends, her family.

Thomas was like a father-figure to her. In his strange way, he had encouraged her to pursue her interests, believed her when she critiqued his inhumane mill, and relied on her to explore chemistry and anatomy when he no longer could. In so many ways, he was a father to her, where her own dad had been more focused on discipline and limitations. She couldn't let her second father die when she had the chance to save him. Not this time. She had been through that pain once. She wouldn't allow it to happen again.

She refused to be a bystander and watch helplessly while people she loved died.

Then there was Andrei.

That tightness came to her chest like a slow boiling pot finally overflowing at the rim. She put a hand to her chest as tears came hot to her eyes, blurring her vision. The fires danced in the oil crevices on the wall, flickering shadows along the wall. Hot tears streaked down Mercy's cheeks and she wiped them away quickly.

"Don't you dare start," she whispered to herself. "If you start now, you won't be able to stop." She clenched her teeth tight and pressed a fist against her chest. She splayed a hand out to the wall, cold stone scraping against the glove she hadn't yet removed. Slowly, she crouched down to her knees, moving her hand down the wall with her.

Shaking, she ordered herself, "Get up." But her limbs wouldn't obey. The thought of Andrei, with his arms and legs bound, tears in his eyes as he faced an array of guns. Andrei, with his body trembling with fear. The horror of it filled her mind, it took hold of her like a clenched fist and she couldn't shake it no matter how hard she tried.

Yes, they were working as a team. Yes, she needed to remind herself she wasn't the only person with something to lose. But she would lose the most. She would lose everything. Again.

Mercy sobbed, covering her mouth with a gloved hand. It wasn't that she was embarrassed, but she didn't want pity. She didn't want their concern focused on her. She would rather they focus on Leyda. Or focus their time on a plan for helping Thomas and Andrei. They didn't have time for this. She didn't have time to shed tears, not when there was so much left to do.

"Mercy?"

Rose. She must have come up the ramp without Mercy hearing it.

With a weak wave, Mercy hoped she got across the

point that she didn't want company. She wanted to be left alone to her fears, alone to her emotions and her pain. But it didn't work.

Rose came closer, crouching down beside her. "Are you okay? What happened?"

Mercy couldn't meet her gaze. The tears just wouldn't stop, no matter how much she tried.

"Hey, it's okay." Rose wrapped her arms around her, pulling her close. The tears came harder. Rose started rocking her. "Do you want to talk about it?"

"I can't stop crying." Mercy sobbed between short gasps. "It's like my heart won't stop hurting. And I don't need this right now. I don't need to feel… weak."

Rose pulled back, pushing hair out of Mercy's face. "There's no shame in crying, and there's no shame in being weak. Nobody says you have to be the leader all the time."

Mercy shook her head, sniffling. "I'm not trying to be the leader. I just want to help everyone. They're my friends, my family!"

Rose gave a small frown. "So, why are you always putting yourself at risk?"

"What?"

Rose winced as though trying to find words. It gave Mercy a moment to catch her breath and wipe at her cheeks. At least the sobbing had stopped for a few minutes.

"Earlier with the Tortoise. You didn't let Kit go first—and for good reason. It definitely didn't feel safe. But instead of talking to either of us, you went and had to go take a look. It was clearly upsetting. The look of the seats…" A shudder went through her. "Awful."

"You saw it?" Mercy asked, wiping at her cheek with her sleeve because her glove was too wet.

Rose nodded, a sad look in her eyes. "I saw some gruesome things when I was living at the werewolf camp. I saw even worse things when I was living as Oscar's pet. That car was probably one of the worst things I've ever seen." She met Mercy's eyes with a piercing gaze. "Why did you feel like you needed to take it all on yourself?"

"I don't know," Mercy said. She thought back to the moment, back to her own protectiveness of Kit. "I've had very bad things happen to me in vehicles. My father was shot beside our car." The tears returned, but she pushed through them. "I fought you back in Oscar's truck. I didn't want Kit to get scarred by what she might see there."

"Ah," Rose smirked. "And you wanted to scar yourself instead?"

"That wasn't it at all," Mercy sighed. "I thought I could handle it. I've experimented on werewolves for over a year. I saw people's corpses get dropped out of windows at Crowsmirth. I've seen people who've been mauled by werewolves. I figured whatever I saw in the Tortoise, whatever horror Leyda was scared of showing us, I figured I could take it."

Rose gave a slow nod. "And now?"

Mercy gave a long sigh. "Now I guess I wasn't ready for it at all."

Rose rubbed a hand on her back. "Look, you're a

brilliant girl and you've done some truly incredible things, but you're still a child."

Mercy groaned.

"No, listen. My point is that you're still a child and shouldn't be so eager to pile everything on your shoulders. Let Kit and I help you. Let us take a few blows now and then. This place is going to beat you down if you don't start sharing the load."

It was tough to hear. Mercy didn't like being reminded of her age. She didn't like to think of her youth because it made her feel unqualified, helpless, and like an impostor. The truth to Rose's words rang true. It wasn't the first time Mercy had thrown herself into danger in order to keep a friend or loved one safe. It wasn't that she was trying to handle it all on her own; it was just easier that way.

"Do you think we would mess things up?" Rose asked.

"No," Mercy thought for a moment. "I think I just assume I'm the most capable." She grinned. "Wow, that sounds bad, doesn't it?"

Rose laughed. "A little. But if I learned anything while staying at your childhood home for so long, Mercy, it's that you were taught to take care of basically everything all the time. Is that about right?"

Mercy nodded, feeling her cheeks get warm.

"You've probably had to do that for most of your life, right?"

She swallowed down the lump in her throat and turned away from those piercing eyes.

Rose chuckled. "I figured. Well, I'm not asking you

to change who you are. All I'm asking is that you share the burden. You know I'm capable. I took care of all of Oscar's messes, remember? And Kit can talk to freaking birds." She laughed, and this time Mercy found herself laughing too.

"And Leyda is a tank," Mercy added with a smile. Rose nodded with a grin.

The pain that had stricken Mercy in the chest had lifted. Even though her eyes felt tired from crying, she felt hopeful for the first time since she and Rose had left her childhood home. Mercy realized she really had been taking on far too much on her own. Other than sending Kit and Rose off to fetch things occasionally, she really hadn't been asking for their opinions much. She had thought she knew best. She had assumed wrongly that they had nothing to impart.

Rose was right. She needed to change. This wasn't her personal revenge and saving mission. Thomas and Andrei weren't her friends alone. They were all friends.

She needed to start treating these people as a team instead of aides on her personal mission. Maybe sharing it all would make it easier to carry. It would surely cut back on her own crying fits. Maybe if she was smart and listened more, they would have a better chance of rescuing their friends. Maybe she would feel less overwhelmed all the time.

Up the stairs came the tinging sound of Kit's footsteps on the metal staircase. Mercy climbed to her feet with Rose's help and prepared to head down to help Leyda.

But this time, she wasn't on her own.

PART 4

7

RECOVERY

MERCY HAD NEVER SEEN Leyda so ravenous. She tore through several large slabs of jerky before downing an entire melon as well. It was as if she hadn't eaten in ages. If she had been down there in the riverbed as long as it seemed, perhaps that explained it.

Finally, she sat covered in a blanket near to the little campsite they had made. Rose sat beside her, holding her hand, a deep look of concern on her face. She hadn't said a word since Kit arrived with the food, but she also hadn't taken her eyes off of Leyda either. Clearly Rose was worried about her.

Mercy approached Leyda slowly, not wanting to alarm her but also curious to see what kind of damage they were dealing with. Leyda hadn't removed her head-scarf or any of the layers of cloth wrapped around her throat and shoulders. If she was still healing from a bad injury, Mercy wanted to know. Maybe she could help. She thought she could at least help with cleaning the wound if there was one. But that required Leyda trusting her.

The only other time Mercy had seen a werewolf terribly injured with a wound that might have killed a normal human was when she first met Andrei. He had been missing an eye. The bad part had been he didn't remember how he lost it. All he knew was that he came out of a transformation and it had been missing. Nightmare fuel for Mercy, but unfortunately a regular occurrence for werewolves. It had taken him over a month to grow it back, but it did grow back. One day, he transformed into his werewolf form and he stared at Mercy with two amber eyes instead of one. It had been unnerving.

"Can I look?" Mercy asked, gesturing to the headwraps and thick scarves on Leyda's head.

Leyda looked at her with heavy eyelids. As if she could have fallen asleep sitting up or leaning against Rose's shoulder. Mercy sympathized with her, but it was clear Leyda needed some kind of help.

"I need to see how bad the damage is."

Leyda's gaze darkened, and she turned away from Mercy. Mercy was afraid she would refuse. For a long moment, she was silent. Finally, she gave a weary sigh before slowly nodding.

Mercy pursed her lips. "I'll be careful, I promise," she said and reached for the headscarf. Leyda didn't acknowledge her, just stared glassy-eyed at the floor. It was like she wanted to be anywhere except here.

Gently Mercy unraveled the wrap. It very loosely lay on top of a thicker scarf in a deep burgundy. Mercy put the loose scarf aside, then started on the second one, only to find it was much harder to move. A knot formed in Mercy's stomach, but she had to help. Even if she wasn't certain if she wanted to see the damage. With the gruesome scene Mercy had seen in the Tortoise, she knew it had to be bad. Leyda was her friend and needed someone to help her. Mercy had the most medical experience.

The scarf had soaked through with blood and hardened in places. It took time for Mercy to find Leyda's hair and fur, to find where her head began and the scarf ended without hurting her. Mercy didn't want to pull some area that was too fragile or too tender. When she finally reached the spot of damage, Mercy's hands began to tremble.

Dried blood had matted Leyda's hair to her scalp, but it was clear that the entire side of her skull had been blown off. No wonder she was still in the process of healing. The skin had stitched back together. Pale scar tissue lay beneath the layers of grime, dirt, and debris. Leyda was lucky to be alive, let alone able to talk to them.

Mercy felt bad for being so clinical earlier when talking to Kit. She felt bad for wanting to press so quickly for information. Once again, she had forgotten to take other people's trauma and emotions into account and she berated herself for it.

She recalled the day Leyda asked for her help in rounding up werewolves around the mill. It had been Mercy's first day working at Farrell Mill. Leyda had been recovering from being shot. Mercy couldn't remember where she had been hit, likely in the head or neck. It had been a straight shot from a pistol so, while the damage was bad, Leyda was healthy and whole at the time. The bullet was expelled from her body over time and the most discomfort she felt was tiredness and a bit of pain. Mercy remembered the sound the bullet made when it was expelled from her body and hit the metal floor at the base of the stairs of the tower.

The bullet had been from Mitchell's pistol. Small, about the size of a fingernail. Whatever had hit Leyda in the head months ago was far worse. A shotgun, maybe. Possibly fired multiple times. She couldn't imagine the pain that would cause, the destruction. Mercy couldn't stop her hands from shaking, though she tried her best to prevent it. This was delicate work, and she didn't want to hurt Leyda more.

"It's bad, isn't it?" Rose asked in a tight voice, as if she was holding back tears. She held onto Leyda's hand so tight her knuckles had blanched.

Mercy nodded and took a moment to find her voice. "Kit, can you fetch some water and a few clean cloths? I... need to clean her up."

"Sure!" Kit was breathless, nervous, even though she was clearly trying not to show it. She hurried off.

Mercy looked at Leyda, who still refused to meet her gaze. "Is talking difficult?" she asked, remembering how she had growled more than talked down at the riverbed.

Leyda gave a short nod.

"But you can say some words still, right?"

She was silent a moment before growling, "Yes."

"Good, I'm glad." Mercy remembered Thomas

explaining how he had originally had to teach Leyda how to talk during the early days of his experimentation. Back when he was first coming to terms with his Liquid Lead and the detrimental effect it had on women. Leyda had to learn to talk despite having more of a snout than a normal face. Mercy was hoping the damage to her head hadn't set her back that much. She honestly wasn't sure if she could help Leyda recover if her injuries were that bad. At least, not without Thomas at her side to assist.

"Here you go!" Kit returned with a bucket of warm water and a small pile of cloths. She also had included a small bar of soap in the bucket. An oversight Mercy had forgotten to request.

Together they worked slowly and meticulously, pulling apart matted hair and fur, scrubbing the scalp and strands with a soapy mixture before drying with a towel. Rose disappeared at one point and came back with a bottle of hair oil. She took up the role of oiling the freshly washed strands. A small luxury to give Leyda at least a little of her dignity back.

Knowing how prideful Leyda usually was, Mercy knew it had to be tough for her to sit there while three women worked on cleaning her wounds, hair, and fur. The whole experience with the Tortoise had to be humiliating. That had to be why she paced in the cave instead of explaining. Or perhaps it was simply too horrible to even try to explain. Either answer was deserved. Leyda had experienced so much pain she deserved any response she had to it.

Leyda didn't complain once throughout the treatment. She seemed grateful. Perhaps the entire ordeal had softened her edges.

As for the cleanup, more than dried blood came out in the water, staining the white bar of soap red. Kit changed out the water three times, all without complaint. Leyda wiped at her eyes once, but Mercy couldn't tell if it was due to tears or exhaustion. Despite the difficulties, all three women worked tirelessly and mostly wordlessly until Leyda's entire head of hair and short fur had been washed and oiled.

Kit shook out her arms once they were done. "Okay, off to go dump this last bucket. Do you need any more water, Mercy?"

"No, I don't think so." Mercy dropped her arms, feeling her biceps ache. Rose finished massaging the remainder of the oil into Leyda's scalp with careful, gentle fingers.

"Are you okay, Leyda?" Mercy asked.

"Hmm?" she mumbled, as if she had been asleep.

"I'm going to take a closer look at the injury now. It may hurt a little. Is that okay?"

Leyda reached a questioning hand up to her hair, feeling the moisturized locks and dragging her fingers through the strands. "Okay," she growled. "Thank you." She wiped at her eyes, and Mercy felt a pang of pity for her.

The hairs parted easily for her now that the area was freshly clean. She had seen some of the impacted scalp while they were working, but now it was much easier to see. The skin itself was healed, but the puckered scarring indicating the where the bullet—or bullets—had erupted was jagged and the scars were red. She pressed fingers against the scar lines, feeling the deep indentions beneath the skin. Leyda flinched.

"Does that hurt?" Mercy asked.

"Yes," Leyda snarled.

Mercy frowned. It was still healing months after the shot. Most of the damage appeared to be at the exit, spreading out like the scatter-shot from a shotgun. Mercy considered herself a pretty good chemist and an amateur biologist when it came to werewolves, but she knew only some about medicine. Worse yet, Leyda wasn't fully a human, and she wasn't fully a werewolf. Mercy had never seen a werewolf injury that took so long to heal. She had no idea why it was still healing.

Could malnutrition be part of it? Would it heal eventually on its own, or should she do something to make it heal faster? She had no idea, and yet she knew she was the best doctor they had on hand. She felt inadequate and terrified at that realization.

Mercy was used to having plans with very clear steps, very carefully marked goals. She was used to being looked up to for her skills and knowledge. But she felt like a novice and an impostor as she stared at the fractured scars along Leyda's scalp.

Mercy had no idea how to help her. If she couldn't help Leyda, what hope did she have of helping Thomas and Andrei?

THE LABORATORY WAS quiet other than the soft snores coming from her friends and the werewolves slumbering inside of their cages. They had all fallen asleep hours ago, shortly after helping clean Leyda and eating dinner, exhausted from the long day. But Mercy couldn't find sleep.

She stared up at the stone ceiling, her mind a whirlwind of nerves, doubt, and panic.

Mercy needed Leyda's help if she hoped to find the many werewolves that had been cured. She needed their help to rescue her friends. In her original plan, she expected to use the Tortoise to collect them, carrying them back here and slowly building a resistance from within the walls of Farrell Mill. The closer the date got to the day of Thomas and Andrei's execution, the more unprepared she felt.

The Tortoise was a mess. It would need major work to get it ready to move people into Kanta. Not to mention she needed stealth when moving people and the Tortoise hadn't been built for stealth. How were they supposed to get people here now? How could they fight against the sheriff and his many hunters if they didn't have the numbers?

Then there was Leyda. She was the linchpin of her plan. Mercy had thought the toughest part would be convincing Leyda to help, but she already had been horribly injured. She had almost been killed inside the Tortoise. They were lucky she was even alive. How could Mercy ask for more from her? How could she ask for her help when Leyda struggled even to even talk?

As much as Mercy hated to admit it, her plan had

fallen apart. She needed a new one, and they only had one more full day to prepare. The firing squad execution was still scheduled for the day after tomorrow.

She had failed.

The realization tore at her. All of that work, that promise, all of it lost. Hot tears fell down her cheeks. Suddenly, she felt small and fragile beneath the tall stone ceiling of the laboratory. She needed to get to her feet. To move. She needed to break away from the sadness threatening to root her in place and pull her downward.

With a grunt, she pushed up to her feet, shoving off the warmth of the blankets and the makeshift bed. Cold pricked at her bare legs and arms, causing gooseflesh. Good. She needed the temperature shock to pull her out of the muck. She breathed in the cold air, allowing it to fill her lungs and shock her body awake. Bending down, she pulled on a pair of woolen socks and covered her feet before she strolled across the laboratory.

For a while she paced, her mind still grappling with the fears that haunted her. A pair of amber eyes caught her attention. Ruth was watching her pace. Mercy walked over to the cage and unlatched it without thinking.

Ruth pricked her ears up with curiosity as Mercy stepped into the cage and crouched down beside her. Her exposed knees shivered as they hit the hay-strewn metal floor of the cage.

"Ruth, I think I've messed up." Mercy's voice cracked. "I put all my faith into a plan, but now it's all falling apart. I—I don't know what to do now." She gripped her elbows, shivering, speaking so quickly her words started to blur together like her thoughts. "I don't know what to do. They're all depending on me. And I know Rose said I need to rely on my friends more, let them help, but I don't know what options we have now. What can we do? What can I possibly do to fix this?"

Ruth cocked her head to the side and shifted, carefully maneuvering her little one so she wouldn't wake up. Her daughter was bigger since the last time Mercy had seen her. Suddenly Mercy felt like she had intruded on a mother and sleeping child, bursting in on someone's private space without warning. She was being rude, barging in on people when they were asleep. That wasn't like her. She shrunk back with shame.

"I'm sorry, I shouldn't have burst in. I'm sorry I bothered you both." She stood to back away. Ruth reached out and put a very large paw on her bare arm. The extended claws pressed lightly against Mercy's skin but did not break the surface.

For a moment, Mercy realized how foolish it was to crawl into the cage with a werewolf. Yes, it was Ruth who seemed to like her—or at least tolerate her to some extent. She had her mind, which made her a thousand times less dangerous than a normal, transformed werewolf. She also was still in the body of a beast who could very easily hurt someone, even if it was accidental. Mercy had gotten the nerve to barge in and be rude.

Not wanting to upset Ruth any further, Mercy lowered herself back the floor until the light claws were removed from her arm. Then to her surprise, Ruth reached her whole arm out and wrapped it around her shoulders, pulling her close. Mercy fell forward more than leaned, and suddenly she was pressed against Ruth's shoulder. She looked down to see Ruth's child, snuggled up against her mother's fur. The child yawned and blinked at Mercy in annoyance, but then she turned over, going back to sleep. Mercy was about to pull away when Ruth dropped her heavy werewolf arm onto her back. Mercy gasped in surprise.

"Okay," she muttered awkwardly. "I guess I did need a hug."

Ruth growled in response, her body vibrating with the low rumble.

Her fur was soft and warm, not coarse like Mercy had expected. No wonder her little one liked to go to sleep against her. It was strange, but it was kind of nice to be hugged by her. It wasn't like Ruth could speak with her, or let her know everything was going to be okay. This was how she communicated, with body language and deep growls and threatening claws. This was how she talked when she couldn't use words. It was strangely comforting. Mercy gave her an awkward hug back, and after a few moments, Ruth released her. Mercy pulled back slowly, careful not to wake the child.

"Thank you," she said. "I needed that."

Ruth snorted hot breath into the chill air and gave a brief nod.

Body language. That was what she used. Suddenly Mercy understood that maybe her plans weren't impossible. Maybe she was panicking. Maybe these fears were due to succumbing to the phantoms that haunted the early mornings and late nights.

Ruth was right. She would be okay. She wasn't

alone. She had help and her plan wasn't a failure; it would merely be different, slowed down perhaps. The steps to her plan hadn't changed. Mercy remembered Rose had even talked about going out early in the morning to help clean up the Tortoise. She had a plan still; it wasn't a failure. She just needed to trust herself and her friends. She had to trust this would work. If not for herself, then at least for Andrei and Thomas.

All it meant was she needed to use her time wisely. That meant getting sleep. It wasn't as if she could do anything at night anyway.

She left Ruth's cage, leaving the door just slightly ajar in case Ruth wanted to stretch her legs.

"I appreciate you believing in me. Even when I struggle to believe in myself."

Ruth gave her a tiny nod, amber eyes not leaving her. Then she nodded her head toward Mercy's makeshift bed with a small grunt.

Mercy chuckled. "I'm going!"

With that, she scuttled over to her bed again and curled beneath the blankets that still held a lingering warmth. She closed her eyes, feeling like a weight had been lifted.

Sleep came quickly like a long-awaited comforter and Mercy welcomed it.

Tomorrow would be a busy day.

8

———————

ASSUMPTIONS

MERCY STARED at the back end of the Tortoise, fear making her stomach do flip-flops. The morning light threw shades of pink and orange onto the ice and snowbanks. It was snowing heavily, and the walk down to the cave entrance had been frigid and treacherous. Mercy felt a lingering ache behind her eyes from her lack of sleep the night before, but she pushed it away.

"Are you ready to do this?" Rose asked, looking between Mercy and Kit. "If you want, I can get started with it and you two can help me out afterwards. I just don't want either of you all touching it until I've gotten the worst of it up."

Kit looked at her with concern. "Are you sure you'll be okay doing that? You've got to pull the thing out of the ice too. That's not going to be easy." She shivered as a gust of wind howled across the riverbed. "Doesn't seem fair."

"I won't be doing it alone. Leyda said she'll help." Rose gestured toward Leyda, who sat on a stool just at the entrance. "Not with the cleanup, but at least with getting it out of the ice."

Leyda was wrapped up in furs, fresh clothes, and scarves, her gaze distant across the riverbed.

"She said that?" Mercy asked. "How does she sound today? Hope she's feeling a little better, at least."

Rose nodded. "She sounded much better to me and seems to feel a lot better too. I think a good few meals and a good night's sleep under warm blankets does wonders. She also seems to be in better spirits."

Working together, Rose and Leyda were able to latch onto two spots on the back of the Tortoise. As a team, they were incredibly powerful. It was unsettling to watch them yank out the giant body of the Tortoise from the thick ice that had encased it into the cave. It broke free with a shudder, followed by several large cracks. Mercy covered her ears at the sound that reverberated in the small space.

They pulled it out onto the flat surface of the riverbed, its wheels still shaking off ice and slushy mud. Mercy couldn't bring herself to look at the front seats or even the front half of the vehicle. Leyda also avoided looking at it, clearly still upset by it.

"You sure about starting it first?" Kit asked, worry in her voice. "Can't I help at all?"

Rose had the front door of the Tortoise open, illuminating the gory mess within with the bright, warm sunshine. Mercy's heartbeat sped up, and she forced herself to turn away from it.

"I tell you what, Kit. You can help me by bringing fresh water and cleaning cloths, okay?"

"Great!" Kit ran off to fetch one of the many buckets of water they had lugged down here.

Mercy went to follow her.

"Not you, Mercy," Rose said.

She arched her eyebrows and turned to look at Rose standing by the open car door. Mercy had to force her eyes to stay on Rose and not flit over to the gore. "What? But you're going to need help."

She shook her head. "I think you've seen enough of this. Go keep Leyda company. I think she needs it."

Mercy pursed her lips. Her instinct was to refuse, but she really didn't want to see that mess again. She wasn't sure what she would do if she had to wipe down the gore from the walls and fabric.

With a heavy sigh, she nodded.

"It's for your own good," Rose said with a small smile. "I promise."

"I know," she said, waving away her concern, then turned to Leyda.

Leyda had settled on a stool at the entrance of the cave and even turned to face the wall of the cave, so she didn't have to see the cleanup. She honestly looked like she did need a friend and Mercy felt bad for her. With a sinking feeling in her gut, Mercy joined her.

"Hey Leyda," she said and cringed at her own over-bright awkwardness. "Mind if I join you?" she asked, lowering her tone.

Leyda glanced toward her, then back to the wall of the cave, giving no indication of an answer.

The sinking feeling deepened.

"I know you and I haven't always seen eye to eye. I

know you get annoyed with my presence most of the time, but I was hoping you could help us with the next stage of the plan."

No response. Mercy curled her fingers into her palms, her stomach doing a series of flops. She got a few steps closer until she was standing right beside Leyda. If Mercy didn't know any better, Leyda looked like she had found a particularly interesting spot of stone on the wall and was incredibly focused on it. Mercy found being treated like she didn't exist irritating.

"Tomorrow they're going to put Thomas and Andrei in front of a firing squad. I was hoping that—"

Leyda cut her off. "I know. Rose explained it all to me this morning." Her voice was gravelly, but far clearer than it had been just the day before. That made Mercy hopeful. Maybe there was a chance after all that they could get this worked out.

"Good, so you already know. We're going to need your help."

"And I'll tell you what I told Rose this morning. I'm not going to be able to help. I'm in no position to do anything, Mercy. I'm sorry, but you're going to have to find someone else."

The pit in Mercy's belly turned into an iciness that flooded her veins. Leyda was the last piece, the final step of a plan she had come so close to giving up on a dozen times already. She didn't need another obstacle, another failure. Leyda had already made her decision without even speaking with her. She had talked to Rose, come to a conclusion, and that was the end of it. Her stubbornness made Mercy want to scream. Instead, she held back her anger and focused on her words.

"You're giving up on them?" Mercy asked, shock and rage tainting her words.

"No," Leyda snarled. "Not giving up! I just know when I can't contribute. I'm useless to you all. I could barely make words yesterday."

Mercy clenched her jaw, her molars clamping together as she fought to keep the scream under wraps that wanted to explode from her. "Leyda," she said as calmly as she possibly could. "You can't do this to us. Not when we're so close. I know you hate me. You've made it clear for years."

Leyda gaped at her as Mercy continued.

"But you can't let this feud between us take the lives of our friends. I won't let you. You can't just throw them away because it's too difficult to work with me. You're the final piece of all of this. You can't do this to us. We need you!"

In a flash, Leyda was on her feet and Mercy took a step backward, panic and adrenaline flooding through her veins.

Leyda put up a palm, halting, and her eyes went wide. "Just hush for a moment, will you? Let me get a word in here? You're twisting things around like you always seem so keen to do. First, I don't hate you. I have never hated you."

Mercy narrowed her eyes. "What? But what about all the things you said about my father? And when you got mad at me for making a cure for Andrei, but it didn't work for you? You've always hated me. Don't lie to me, Leyda."

Leyda blinked, then shook her head. "Mercy, just because I'm angry doesn't mean I hate you. Believe it or not, I was trying to fix our friendship for a while. I felt like once you met Andrei, you didn't want to be friends with me anymore. As if I was too difficult to be friends with. As if I was too ugly… to befriend." She gave a shaky sigh, a white puff of condensation expelling from her muzzle. "I realize I'm a difficult person. I have anger issues. I struggle, but I do try to keep them in check. I don't know if you believe me or not, but I don't hate you, Mercy." She barked a bitter laugh. "If anything, I feel like I have failed you again and again."

Mercy stared at her in disbelief.

"I forgot to go back for you the night you had to shoot Henry. That was entirely my fault. Then when they came to take Andrei and Thomas, I knew I failed you again. That's why I went back to get the Tortoise. I knew Thomas had some of your cure hidden in there as an emergency supply. If the sheriff and his lackey got their hands on that, I wasn't sure what they would do. That was what I knew I had to protect. I took care of Kit, my fellow werewolves, and I made sure the cure stayed out of their hands."

Mercy reached out and took Leyda's arm, wanting to shake her. "They could have killed you!"

She smiled in her distorted way. "I know, and they almost did. But they didn't, did they? Just because you make me so mad I can't see straight sometimes doesn't mean I don't admire you. And I'll do whatever it takes to keep you and that brilliant mind of yours safe. That includes your cure too."

Mercy let out a slow breath, taking a moment to let Leyda's words fully sink in. All this time, she had assumed Leyda hated her. She had assumed every slight was personal. Every word or glance intentional. Even Andrei tried to pull her back from making assumptions about Leyda when she had gone too far. Everyone had seen the obvious truth, but Mercy had been too close to see. She had been too intent on making everything Leyda said personal instead of understanding the pain and daily torment her friend was going through. It went against everything she thought she knew about the woman, but it also made more sense too. That's how she knew Leyda was speaking the truth.

"I'm sorry," Mercy whispered, her tongue too clumsy to get out the words. How could she fully apologize for a wrong that had lasted so long? She tried again. "I'm sorry I didn't understand. I made it all about me instead of listening to you more."

Leyda shrugged. "We're all fighting our own battles, Mercy. I just wish I could help you with this next one."

Mercy raised an eyebrow in confusion. "So you do want to help us?"

"Of course I do!" She scoffed. "You think I want to see them gunned down by a firing squad? But I can't. It's not my strength. I feel like I could shove that Tortoise a dozen feet with one arm. No, it's my mind. It feels... disconnected, like it's floating behind me sometimes, trying to catch up. It's a little better since I found you all. I forgot what it was like to talk, to have friends around. I've been alone out here for months, but it felt like years sometimes."

Mercy nodded, finally understanding what Leyda meant. At first, she had been outraged by Leyda choosing to leave her friends behind at the mill, for locking Kit up in the laboratory and abandoning her, but now she understood. Mercy hadn't been listening, just making assumptions. She shook herself, wondering if she had done the same thing to any of her other friends.

"I don't need you there," Mercy said. "I just need what you know. Do you remember the werewolves we gave the cure to? The ones you took out of Kanta so they could create new lives?"

She grinned, "Of course I do! I was so proud of you that I couldn't stop telling them about you. I may have said a little too much at times, but we had information to hold over them, so it felt safer to prattle on."

A pang of regret spread like a wound across Mercy's chest. She remembered sitting on the catwalk and watching those cured werewolves wave up at her in appreciation. Mercy had assumed Leyda had told them about her as a way to get back at her, as a way to back-stab her. In actuality, Leyda had been praising her and bragging about her the entire time. She hadn't even seen that. Once again, she just had thought it was another way Leyda had hurt her, made Mercy suffer for some unknown injustice.

"I have misunderstood you for so long and I'm so very sorry," Mercy said, moving to take Leyda's hand and squeezing it tight.

Leyda snorted. "To be honest, I think we both have. I've never treated you that well. I sometimes have problems saying what I mean to." She laid her other hand over Mercy's. "I've been cruel to you. Sometimes even petty, and I really shouldn't have. If you have a bad perception of me, it's also my fault." She gave a heavy sigh. "So let's both try to be more patient with each other in the future."

Mercy nodded, feeling the shame slowly lift from her shoulders. "Let's do that."

Leyda released her hand and sat up straighter on her stool. "So tell me, what information do you need? I can help with the information. I just don't think I can go into a field and fight your hunters for you. I'm in no position for that, not like this. I could possibly hurt someone if I'm put into a corner, but strategy and planning are out of my field at the moment."

Mercy held up her hands, laughing. "I don't need all of that! I certainly don't want to put you in a corner somewhere. I just need to know where we can find the werewolves we cured. I'm hoping I can call them in as favors, get them to come to Kanta and help us take down the firing squad."

Leyda leaned back, shaking her head and crossing her arms. "You need all of them? I don't think we need that many people to get Thomas and Andrei out of jail, Mercy. And I think attacking before the firing squad is a much better idea. Fewer guns to take down."

Mercy shook her head. "We need as many people on our side as we can get."

Leyda frowned. "Why?"

"Because we aren't just freeing our friends." She looked around, trying to find the right words, hoping she was on the right path. She hadn't told her plan to anyone, not even Kit and Rose. They knew pieces, but they didn't know everything. Here she was about to divulge it all to Leyda and hope that it would be enough to convince her to help. After struggling for too long to find the right words, Mercy finally just poured it out bluntly.

"We're going to take Kanta back. And we'll kick out anyone who opposes us."

Her eyes went wide. "But Mercy… that would turn Kanta into…"

Mercy nodded and smiled. "A werewolf sanctuary."

Leyda gaped at her.

"Now, I know it sounds crazy, but imagine it. No more having to hide. No more disguises. No more hunters kidnapping women or killing werewolves in the street."

Leyda narrowed her eyes. "What if a werewolf stumbles into town—like Henry did?" Leyda asked, her tone conspiratorial.

"Everybody has a cure on them. Everyone has a stash. A dozen werewolves who can transform at will to corral and cure anyone who comes in." Mercy gave her a hard stare. She had already thought of so many options, so many possibilities. It was one of the reasons she had trouble sleeping so often.

Tears sprang up in Leyda's eyes. Mercy hoped that was a good sign.

"I've been thinking about this for a long time,"

Mercy admitted. "Think of the growth Kanta would have, the number of werewolves and victims of trafficking who would come here for safety. They would come here for refuge. Kanta has no official mayor anymore. Did you know that?"

Leyda shook her head slowly, still gaping at her.

"Thomas let it slip one day. I think that's why the sheriff can do whatever he likes. But it means that if we chase out every person who calls themselves part of Kanta's infrastructure—the sheriff, the lieutenant, and anyone else who wants to be part of their mob—we can claim this city as ours. We can found a new city in whatever form we want. Populated by cured werewolves and werewolf sympathizers."

Tears streamed down Leyda's cheeks. "Mercy… that would be beautiful."

"It's possible, Leyda. This isn't just a dream. But I will need you to help us gather them. You've actually spoken to them. Do you think they would return for us?"

Leyda dropped her gaze and furrowed her brows, her mind lost in thought for a moment before she answered. "I think if they knew what you were planning, if they fully understood what you wanted to create, they would come back in droves. I don't think we would be able to keep them out. They would want to come here that badly."

In Mercy's mind, the tiny seed of the plan she had planted before finally had its first flower.

"So you will help us find them?"

"Find them?" Leyda smiled. "I'll go tell them to pack up and bring any weapons they have. But Mercy, if we do this, if we take over Kanta, we might make enemies elsewhere. Those lords up north might get angry. They could send hunters, or even troops, to kill us."

Mercy nodded. "That's true. But when Crowsmirth got annihilated, they didn't care about the townspeople. They just saw an opportunity to kill a lot of werewolves and make a profit. It was a huge group of werewolf hunters, but those numbers will pale compared to the werewolves we've helped. They will be living like people here, not as werewolves. To any outsiders it looks like a regular town, not a werewolf sanctuary."

Leyda grinned. "The more we talk about this," she said, bouncing her leg, "the sooner I want to get started."

"Well..." Mercy pulled out her journal, pen, and ink bottle from her satchel. "I brought this in case I needed to take field notes. But you can start making lists of the cured werewolves and where to find them."

"Excellent!" Leyda cried, grabbing the materials and starting in.

Mercy smiled as she watched Leyda scribble down names and addresses. Maybe her idealized plans weren't so terribly far-fetched after all. Maybe there was some chance, however small, for Kanta to be fully transformed. For a city that had been home to so many injustices, it would be good to see justice done for all those who had been wronged.

This had to work. For her friends and for a new weird and strange Kanta that might just come true.

PART 5

9

A SECOND FAMILY

IT HADN'T TAKEN them long to clean out the Tortoise once Rose was done with the first sweep. Between Kit, Rose, and Mercy working together, they had it finished within hours. The sun wasn't quite at its zenith when they poured out the remainder of their water and disposed of the dirty cloths.

"It looks great!" Rose proclaimed as she did the final inspection. "It doesn't even smell anymore. You were right about the cleaners to use, Kit."

Kit grinned. "I had to clean up all sorts of messes back at my old house. If there's one thing I know, it's how to clean bloodstains out of fabric. Especially when it came to werewolf bloodstains."

Leyda winced and gave Kit a sidelong look.

"Oh uh, sorry, Leyda. I guess that was a little insensitive."

Watching her friends, Mercy shook her head.

"You should check it out, dear." Rose gestured to Leyda. "It looks a lot better."

Leyda gave a little huff before letting Rose help her into the Tortoise. "It… actually looks wonderful." She pushed around the seats before hopping out again and turning to Mercy.

"So, Rose and I need to get going if we're going to reach as many people as we can before daybreak. Is that right?"

Mercy nodded. "Probably a good idea. Every minute we lose more daylight and more time. Do you have the food and water skins we prepared?"

Leyda nodded as she went around to the passenger side. "Come on, Rose, you're driving. I don't trust myself with anything this dangerous. Knowing my luck, we would go straight into a river or a tree."

"Wait, aren't we going with them?" Kit asked, looking between Mercy and the Tortoise as Rose climbed into the driver's seat.

"Afraid not, Kit. You and I have a lot of work to finish up here first." Mercy unholstered her gun and handed it through the window to Rose. "Here, take this. Just in case. You don't know what you're going to run into out there. Or who. And remember, you can't let anyone see you transform."

"Don't worry, I'm not interested in transforming into anything for a while after the mess we ran into last time. That was exhausting, and Leyda needs me to be able to drive us back home. I don't want to wear myself out." She looked at the gun in Mercy's hands and winced. "Only regular bullets, I hope. No silver."

"You sure?" Leyda asked. "I say we take both. If

we're out after dark, I don't want to get killed because you're squeamish."

"And how do we load them?" Rose asked with a glare.

"With gloves on. But if they save our lives, then it's worth the trouble."

Rose grunted. "Seems dangerous, but whatever." She turned back to Mercy. "Give me all of them."

Mercy pulled the pouch of bullets off her belt and handed them over. "Just be careful. Remember, it's at noon tomorrow, so we need everyone at the rendezvous point by morning."

"I know," Leyda snarled, pulling on gloves before taking the gun and bullets. "And Thomas already ran me through all the ridiculous features on this thing. That was another reason I knew I had to get it out of there and keep it from the sheriff."

Rose reached over, pulled over Leyda's arm, and planted a kiss on the back of her hand. "Always one step ahead of them, my love."

Leyda blinked and snarled something inaudible, making Rose laugh.

Mercy backed away from the Tortoise. "Be careful. We'll see you both back tomorrow."

"Yeah, we better," Kit said. "Don't make me have to go looking for you. My bird friends will not be nice about it. They will peck and it will hurt."

Rose chuckled. "Understood. You two stay low if you can." She waved. "See you soon. Wave, dear."

Leyda gave a halfhearted wave and rolled her eyes. "Fine."

Mercy and Kit waved after them as the Tortoise sped off over the snow and ice down the riverbed. Supposedly, a ramp down there led up to the back roads on the outskirts of Kanta. Mercy had to trust they knew what they were doing and she, in fact, didn't need to know all the details of every part of this plan. It was scary, but she had come to realize that trust was sometimes scary. Relying on other people to not let her down, to fulfill their promises, and to do what they said they would, was scary.

Slowly she was realizing her upbringing meant she had a harder time trusting. She had a harder time believing people, even when they were being honest with her. She had been told several times she needed to accept help, but Mercy had a hard time asking for or receiving help. It was something she had started working on. As the Tortoise disappeared from view over the horizon, she felt a swell of pride in herself. Today was a big step forward.

Andrei would be proud of her. The realization made her heart ache.

"So why couldn't we go with them, Mercy? I was looking forward to helping them rally everybody."

Mercy took a deep breath, the icy air chill on her throat. The sun was almost at its peak in the sky and trickles of water dripped along the walls of the riverbed. It must have finally reached above freezing for a little while. "Because we have to plan for tomorrow. Rose and Leyda will rally the people, but we have to give them instruction when they get here. We have to give them supplies and provide backup."

"Oh," Kit muttered, all the excitement draining from her voice.

"Think you can wrangle some of your birds for me? We'll need their help, too."

Kit blinked. "Sure, no problem."

IT TOOK LONGER to freshen up than Mercy liked. She was getting used to moving around the mill, especially now she knew where the drainage pipes were and how to move around undetected. She last saw Kit when they were grabbing a bite to eat in the kitchen. As Kit went off to gather her birds, Mercy went to fetch a fresh pistol and bullets from her office in the laboratory. Kit had told her to meet on the roof. Mercy had agreed, but hadn't really understood what that meant.

Was there access to the roof? If so, where was it?

She had already walked around the upper floors of the tower three or four times and was beginning to get annoyed. Why did they have to meet on the roof anyway? Couldn't the crows fly anywhere Kit asked them to? She felt like she was wasting time again and it frustrated her.

"Over here!" Kit called. Mercy jumped. She turned to see Kit standing in the window on the backside of the tower, her hands on either side of the window frame as one leg swung back and forth.

Panic leapt into Mercy's throat and she scrambled over to her side. "Kit! What are you doing? You're going to fall."

As she got closer, Kit hopped backward, the sound Mercy heard meant that the girl's feet had landed on something metal.

Alarm turned into confusion. Mercy blinked. "What?"

"It's the fire escape," Kit said proudly. "I found it when I was trying to sneak around the mill. Didn't you know it was here? If a fire had broken out, you would have been trapped."

Mercy put her head out the window and eyed the metallic landing, along with the series of metal landings and ladders beneath it. She had never noticed this existed, and she had considered herself an experienced worker at the mill. Come to think of it, Thomas had mentioned a fire escape in passing once, but Mercy had assumed he was talking about some new invention or contraption, not an actual fire escape.

"It's a good thing I'm here to teach you about these things. Now you're way more prepared for a fire. Come on." Kit started up the ladder bolted into the wall beside the window. She moved quickly.

Mercy climbed out onto the metal landing and looked up at the ladder. It was long like the ladders that led down to the grinders. Clearly Thomas had a thing for ridiculously long ladders. It did look like it led to the roof though, and Kit was already near the top. Mercy double-checked to make sure her pistol, knife, and bullets were properly attached to her hip. She tightened her leather gloves. Then she started climbing.

The wind picked up as she climbed, shrieking

against the metal grommets and bolts of the building. It made her teeth chatter, and she shivered against it. By the time she got to the top, her face stung from the chill.

A clear blue sky stretched out before her, dotted with white puffy clouds. Below it, the forest stretched out in almost every direction. For the first time, Mercy could see how isolated Kanta was. A few roads made up the city and a few overgrown dust trails led out of town. But that was it.

Way up here, the message was clear: no visitors wanted. From up here, it was clear, too, that every single building in Kanta revolved around werewolf trapping. From the pub to the hotel to the jail, everything was about werewolves and using them to make money. Now that Mercy understood the true trade that flowed beneath the werewolf trapping, she saw how easily Kanta could be used for human trafficking too.

But it hadn't always been that way. That was clear from the dried-up riverbed and the enormous water-wheel on the side of the mill. Seeing it from above, at a vantage point she had never even considered before, Mercy understood why Kanta had such a hard time changing. It was perfectly built and situated to resist change. Unless somebody took a big risk to upset that perfect balance, it was built to be impervious to it.

Mercy swallowed down the lump in her throat as she realized just how difficult her plan was going to be. A pit of worry formed in her stomach as regret pulled at her. Maybe Kit was right. Maybe they should have gone with Leyda and Rose. Maybe gathering people here was more important than she had first assumed. She hoped she hadn't underestimated the hunters and officers they were going up against.

"See all of my friends?" Kit asked.

Mercy had been so engrossed with the view she had missed Kit moving off to the side. She gestured with excitement at the flock of birds behind her.

Kit had said she had a few bird friends, but Mercy counted at least forty crows. "There are so many," Mercy said. She gaped at how calmly the flock sat on the roof, not at all bothered by the humans present. They were so calm, it was unsettling.

"I know! I asked for my friends to come join me on the roof for a super secret plan, but then they brought their friends and even their family with them. I never expected them to want to help me so much. But I think they appreciated that we stopped Leyda from throwing rocks at them."

Kit came over to take her hand, leading her to the side, away from the ledge and the ladder.

"Stay over here, okay? I don't know if anybody really looks up here very often, but I don't want to risk it."

As they moved to the side, Mercy noted how the curvature of the roof hid almost all of Kanta from view. She couldn't imagine anyone really looking up this high, but then again, even if they did, she doubted they would see much. All the same, Kit was right, better safe than sorry. They couldn't risk getting caught now, not when they were so close to ending this.

"How do I talk to them?" Mercy asked, gesturing to the birds. "Does it have to be in crow or something?"

Kit laughed. "Like you talk to anybody else. Crows are really smart. They'll understand. And if they look confused, I'll help clarify."

"Okay…" Mercy looked doubtfully at the birds, who seemed only interested in preening, chatting together, or falling asleep. "I don't know what I was expecting. I guess I thought they would be more attentive?"

Kit sighed. "They can hear you. Try to be nice, okay? These are my friends."

Mercy winced. "Sorry. I'm doing my best."

Kit gestured again to the crows. "Don't apologize to me—apologize to them!"

Taking a deep breath, Mercy turned back to the crows, only to see dozens of tiny black eyes fixed on her. It was alarming, especially since they hadn't seemed to care about her before. Was it Kit who got their attention, or was it just that the crows were almost supernatural? Or maybe Mercy had just insulted them that badly already.

She cleared her throat and took a step toward the flock. None of them flew back or even looked away from her. Mercy steeled herself, then said, "I didn't mean to offend you. I'm sorry about that. I'm still getting used to you all understanding me."

A few of the birds flapped their wings, but Mercy didn't know what that even meant. Kit didn't interrupt her or ask her to back down, so she assumed it wasn't a bad sign. Mercy continued, "Tomorrow at noon—"

"That means high sun!" Kit explained, putting her hand flat into the sky.

The birds looked at Kit and then back at Mercy again.

The hairs went up on the back of Mercy's neck. She licked her lips and kept going. "The people below are going to try to kill my friends." Her throat constricted, but she kept going. "Thomas is like a father to me. He took me in when my dad was killed. He saved my life. He may not be perfect or always a very good person, but he's my friend. He taught me. He's helped so many people. I can't see him shot. I can't see him down on the ground with the light out of his eyes like Henry or Oscar or those people in Crowsmirth. I just can't."

Tears filled her eyes as she took a deep breath and prepared herself for the hardest part. "Andrei is with him. He's a good person. Like an actually good person, not damaged like me. He's always trying to help people. It's a part of who he is. It's one of the reasons I love him so much. He's selfless, humble, smart, cute as hell, and he's going to die tomorrow unless I get your help. Please help us. I don't know if you like me like you like Kit. I don't even know if you understand a word I'm saying." She squeezed her eyes shut as tears fell down her cheeks. "Please. I don't have any other options."

A warm hand slipped into hers and she opened her eyes to Kit standing beside her, tears in her eyes. "Oh Mercy, I don't want them to die either."

They hugged. Kit gripped her with desperation, as if the reality of their mission had finally fallen upon her. Mercy hated that Kit was stuck in this with her.

Hated the people who hurt her loved ones. Hated Kanta and the corruption that had the city in an iron grip.

Mercy gently pulled away from Kit, anger sweeping past her sadness and fear. "What do you say?" she asked the birds. "Will you help us?"

Dozens of eyes stared at her, but once again Mercy wasn't sure if any of what she said was making it through. All she saw were those black, emotionless eyes, and all the anger that filled her started to fizzle out on the edges.

She held her palms out to them. "So what will it be, my feathered friends? Will you help me save my second father and the man I love?"

A cold wind swept past and Mercy caught the scent of pines, earthy leaves, and the distant smoke of a fireplace. The birds seemed agitated, and she prepared for them to fly off, rejecting her and the mission. If that happened, she wasn't sure what they would do. Despite her fears, she tried to calm herself and waited for their judgment.

One of the bigger crows in the front spread their wings wide and cawed loudly at her. Mercy jumped. With a few flaps, it leaped into the air and landed awkwardly on her arm.

"Ah!" Mercy cried as wide wings flapped chaotically in her face and the bird's claws bit into her outstretched arm.

"Hold still, Mercy! This is a good sign."

"Is it?" she asked, heart pounding fast in her chest.

Another bird flew up to her, landing awkwardly on

her other arm. They were heavier than they looked and very awkward as they tried to balance on her.

"They're accepting you into the fold." Kit was shaking her arms with excitement, but all Mercy felt was pain in her forearms as their talons tried to get a purchase on her.

Half a minute passed before the two birds gained their balance. Mercy had a moment to catch her breath and feel like she was getting the hang of this when the rest of the flock flew at her.

One moment they were all watching her, fluffing their feathers and chattering among themselves, and the next they were airborne and flying at her. Suddenly they blotted out the sky, the sunlight, and even Kit.

Mercy cried out, then shut her eyes and clamped her mouth closed. Wings beat against her, feathers grazed her cheeks, and claws scraped lightly against her skin. She opened her eyes briefly, seeing black feathers everywhere. She was scared to even breathe.

Then they began cawing.

It was so loud she winced at the pain in her ears. Then the birds flew off of her in an enormous gust. The two birds launched off of her at the same time, knocking her backward to land on her rear.

She grunted as she fell, staring up at the cloud of crows as they circled above their heads. It was surreal. Their formation reminded her of a leaf on the wind, shifting and dancing on the breeze. They were so much bigger in person than she had ever imagined when seeing them in trees, especially when they were using her as a perch.

Kit was at her side in an instant, pulling her to her feet. "You're shaking," she said. "Are you okay? I've never seen them flock like that before. Well… I guess I have, but only once before."

"When?" Mercy had a million questions, but the word sprang from her trembling lips without a second thought.

Kit bit her bottom lip, avoiding making eye contact with her. She didn't respond and that flare of anger sparked up in Mercy again. "Kit, where have you seen them flock like that before? Am I in danger? Please tell me they're not going to turn around and swarm me like they did that guy in Crowsmirth."

Kit looked at her, worry on her face. "When I asked them to attack someone for me. They're very protective of me. I don't really know why, but they are."

Mercy blinked. "They're going to attack me?"

"No—they'll attack whoever you want them to."

Mercy fell silent, watching the birds again. The flock of crows flew low again, cawing in a cacophony in the clear blue sky. "A murder of crows," Mercy whispered.

"They sure seem like it."

Mercy took a deep breath, wiping the dirt and feathers off of her coat. She wasn't shaking as badly now. They hadn't hurt her—not terribly, at least. She wiped a small trickle of blood away from beneath her left eye and looked wryly down at the scratches on her arms.

"So, are they going to help us tomorrow? That's all I need to know."

"Definitely," Kit said, transfixed by the flock above their heads.

Mercy raised an eyebrow. "But I haven't given them any instructions. How will they know what to do when the time comes? How will they know what I want them to do?"

Kit smiled. A gleam came to her eyes that was slightly unsettling. "They're birds, Mercy. And they've accepted you now. You're a part of their flock. You told them who your family is. They'll figure it out. All you have to do is give them direction tomorrow, and they'll do as you ask. They like you. They'll try to help. I don't know if you fully understand what this means though."

Mercy blinked at her as a frigid wind swept over the rooftop. "Wait, there are strings attached? You didn't mention that."

Kit shrugged. "It's not a big deal. Just help them like they help you. They might have to give their lives for you. They expect you to try to do the same for them too. It's a mutual agreement. You help each other out."

"Oh." Mercy stared at her. "I wish you had said that before."

"Would you have done it if I had?" Kit grinned.

"No… probably not."

Kit stretched, pulling her arms above her head. "It's just an agreement, Mercy. Consider them like a second family for you now."

Mercy considered that. A second family of crows. What did that even mean?

Kit held up a finger. "But don't betray their trust. They will not like you if you do that. And they'll turn on you. They have a hard time trusting humans as it is, you know? Don't be the person that makes them decide to give up on us entirely."

The flock swayed off toward the forest. Mercy watched them until they disappeared amid the tree branches.

"I guess that makes two of us."

10

EVERYTHING CHANGED

THE SUN CREPT FAR TOO QUICKLY into the sky. Mercy hadn't gotten much sleep because she was so anxious. For the second night in a row, she'd had trouble sleeping. If everything worked out the way she hoped, maybe she wouldn't be alone this evening. Maybe she would have Andrei with her and she wouldn't have to feel so scared for him anymore.

She tightened her hands on the metal railing of the spiral staircase. This wasn't the time to be hopeful or foolish. She needed to focus on her plan. No, on their plan. And trust her friends would be able to pull this off. She had to trust in her team.

At the base of the spiral stairway in the tower, Mercy checked herself. She had a sack filled with every gun she could find in the mill. Each was cleaned, tested, and had a matching bag of ammunition. After she and Kit had finished with the strange business with the crows, they had gone down to search for any useful supplies.

Mercy had prepped the guns and ammunition just

as she used to for her father a lifetime ago. Kit prepared the food. Mercy wasn't sure how, but she had said she found food she could prepare. Having been kept as a servant in the house with her previous captors for years, she had gotten good at cooking and preparing dried goods for travel.

Basically, she and Mercy were preparing for troops, werewolf and sympathizers alike, to help overthrow Kanta today. They had no idea how many people were coming, if any at all. Even though Mercy had stayed awake as long as possible, through a mixture of insomnia and nerves, she had never seen Rose or Leyda return. A thousand worries filled her mind overnight, and it had been a struggle to push them away when the dawn arrived.

But she had to. Andrei needed her.

Satisfied with her preparations, she heard the tinging of Kit's footsteps against metal as she descended the staircase. Like Mercy, she carried a large bag on her back filled with supplies. She looked tired as she made it to the bottom of the stairs.

"You really think anybody is coming?" Kit asked. "I made a bunch of food, but I worry. Especially since we haven't heard anything from Leyda or Rose." She shifted the bag so it sat over her shoulders.

"They'll come," Mercy said, encouraging herself as much as Kit. "We have to trust that they got through."

Kit bit her lip, her gaze distant. "I hope you're right."

Together they went for the door that led down to the bellows. It was still pitch black down there, but they had started getting used to the darkness. Mercy dragged her hand along the hewn stone, counting doors. One, two, and finally three. She pushed the door open, flooding the narrow hall with light and had to shield her eyes.

She held the door open for Kit, already setting her own expectations of what they would find. "If no one comes, we can at least put the food aside for later. I doubt that the four of us can eat it all, but at least we won't all starve if this falls through."

Kit rushed past her, darting to the edge and the long drop beyond the waterwheel. Mercy held her breath, hoping for an exclamation, but Kit's long silence made her stomach drop. Swallowing down the sudden dryness in her throat, Mercy pushed the door closed behind them. She took her time walking over to stand on the ledge beside Kit. What she saw tore her breath away.

All along the riverbed were parked vehicles. People walked around, chatting, and even a few children played in the distance. It wasn't just a few who had answered their call, there were dozens of them. Quickly, Mercy counted off the people she saw who weren't holed up in vehicles. Her mouth dropped open as the number kept going up.

"Over fifty of them." Mercy gasped. "I didn't know if we would get one, let alone fifty!"

Kit jumped up and down on the ledge, her hands gripping the spindle of the massive defunct waterwheel.

"They came!" she cried. "I can't believe it! Oh, I owe some rations to Leyda and Rose when I see them. They deserve double rations for this."

Mercy scanned the riverbed before spotting it. The

Tortoise was at the far end, beside the playing children, off at a distance.

"They made it!" Mercy whispered, realizing in that moment how much she had feared never seeing them again.

With matching grins, Mercy and Kit exchanged a look before racing down to the riverbed. When they reached the bottom, they ran into a fairly large crowd of people waiting at the base of the incline.

Reunions would have to wait. These people needed time to prepare and guidance on what to do. If they messed up the timing, people would die. She had no illusions about that.

"Mercy!" Leyda called.

Mercy spun around a couple of times before spotting them both. Leyda had her headwrap off, which was so unusual for her that Mercy froze on the spot. Rose wrapped her arms around Mercy's waist and picked her up off the ground in a big hug.

Her bag of guns clattered to the ground, but Mercy didn't care. She was too busy relishing that these two, her friends, had made it back safe and sound.

"I was afraid you all had been captured," she admitted when Rose put her back onto the ground and she retrieved her bag.

"I didn't doubt for a minute you two would make it!" Kit said.

Rose laughed. "We had to camp out in the Tortoise overnight, but that was the worst of it. I forget how intense transformed werewolves can be. They were way worse than Silver and Jamison."

Mercy looked between them. "Were there many of them? Did you get hurt? Did the electric fence on the Tortoise work?"

Leyda crossed her arms as Rose shook her head. "I told you not to mention the werewolves. The girl's mind is a steel trap for anything lycanthropy." She gave Mercy a smile. "We were fine. Thomas built it to be a tank, and it certainly felt like one." A sparkle came to her eyes as she drew closer. "I think these people have come a long way to see you. Don't you think you should introduce yourself and let them know the plan?"

Mercy blinked in confusion. They came a long way to see her? She didn't understand. They came to liberate Kanta, right? Not listen to her.

Something tugged out of her hand. Kit was pulling the gun bag away from her. "I'll take care of this. You go talk to your fans."

"My fans?" Mercy asked helplessly. She realized the crowd had parted around her and all eyes were focused on her. But how did they know who she was? Oh wait, Leyda had called out to her. She and Rose had probably given them a quick summary about who she was, what she had created, and what to expect. She remembered that pair—possibly a father and son—from ages ago at the base of the grinder, bowing to her, thanking her from a distance.

They were fans, she realized with horror. Just like these people. They were all fans of her work.

Heat flooded her cheeks and her tongue glued stubbornly to the roof of her mouth. Her hands shook as sweat broke out on the back of her neck. This was a hundred times worse than facing down a transformed werewolf.

Leyda elbowed her not too gently in the side and that was the movement that broke her from her mute terror.

"Thank you all for coming," she said, her voice too soft and way too shaky. She cleared her throat and tried again. "I appreciate every last one of you." That was better. Now she just had to figure out where she was going. The flock of crows came to mind from the rooftop of the mill. She thought of the words she had spoken to them, the truth she had voiced up there. She knew what she had to say, even though it would be diffi-cult. She cleared her throat and her voice felt free again.

"This might be common knowledge by now, but my friends are currently being held captive at the jail." More people stepped into the crowd to listen, to learn. She pushed the fear down and continued.

"Today, they're to be killed by a firing squad. Why? Because they helped distribute the cure to you all. Because they helped you start a new life. I am asking—pleading—for your help today. I've realized I can't do this on my own, but maybe together we can set it right."

Murmuring among the crowd mixed with worried faces. They were sort of on board, she realized, but not quite interested in risking or exposing themselves to fully help. They were curious, but they hadn't decided yet. She couldn't blame them for that. What she was asking them to do was dangerous. Mercy knew if she didn't sway their minds, Andrei would be face down in a puddle of his own blood come noon.

"Maybe you should introduce yourself?" Leyda asked, eyeing her warily. "Why should they help you?"

Mercy's hands shook. She didn't want to tell them, but Leyda was right. Some might not know who she is. Maybe she had been presumptuous in assuming Leyda and Rose had explained everything. These people had come a long way. They needed to know why she was here if she hoped to get their help. "My name is Mercy Pinkerton, the daughter of Solomon Pinkerton."

Cries of outrage and anger echoed back at her. She expected that, but it still hurt.

"The reason you are able to exist at night without transforming is because of the cure I made. I created the partial cure that freed you from having to transform every night."

A hush fell over them, and suddenly Mercy didn't feel threatened or overwhelmed. She felt connected to these people. Every one of them had been helped because of her. They were all standing here, healthy and alive, because of her. She tried not to dwell on that thought too long because she might fall apart again.

"This city has taken everything from me. It took my mother when I was born. It took my father, who only wanted to keep me safe. Now it's taken my second father, Thomas, who many of you have met. His passion for this work is why you all have the freedom to go back and live comfortable lives of anonymity." She took a shaky breath. "They've also taken Andrei, my boyfriend, who is a cured werewolf like each of you. If he gets shot and lives today, your secret is out. They'll kill him with silver and your lives won't be safe any longer. They'll know you exist. Either way, the secret is out today, but I think we can do more good by showing them that we mean business, instead of letting them steal another werewolf's life away."

The audience was silent as a cold breeze swept freshly blooming flower petals across the riverbed. Mercy wiped the tears from her eyes and kept going. Anger filled her, and she spat out her next words like a chant to the crowd.

"I am tired of Kanta always taking everything from me. I am tired of it ripping my life and my loved ones away. The fear we live in everyday doesn't have to define us. Imagine living in Kanta as you are, fully embracing both your humanity and lycanthropy. Imagine feeling free to raise your kids here, regardless of sex. No more hiding. No more slinking in the shadows and hiding from hunters."

Someone cheered, followed by another and another. The cries filled Mercy's heart to the brim.

"Help me take Kanta back for its rightful people. Help me take down these hunters, these kidnappers, and these murderers. Together, we can kick them out of Kanta and take this city back as ours!"

Cheers erupted from the crowd. It was as if Mercy unplugged a faucet and fast moving water rushed out in a torrent. She held up her hands to get them quiet, and to her amazement, they were.

"Now listen up! We can't rush in with guns blazing. I want my friends saved, not killed in the crossfire."

Mercy laid out the plan. To her astonishment, when

she finished, she saw the same fire and determination in their eyes that she felt in her heart.

———

THE SHADOWS WERE short as Mercy made her way out onto Main Street. She had her hair up, along with a big hat and a bandanna wrapped around her mouth and nose. It didn't feel nearly as effective as the wolf helmet or the face wrappings, but Leyda assured her she was "good enough." Mercy wasn't sure if she was right or if Leyda just wanted to hurry her along so she could help other women blend into the front lines. Mercy was pleased to see there were a lot of people there waiting for Leyda's help.

All of Kanta flooded the street, almost every one of them a man other than a few older women scattered amid them. Mercy couldn't remember ever hearing of a firing squad executing people in Kanta, but the new sheriff clearly wanted to make a name for himself. What better way to do that than to kill the richest man in town in front of everyone?

Amid the crowd, she spotted members of their resistance group. Some blended so well with the people of Kanta that Mercy couldn't always be sure if they were one of them or not.

A crow cawed above and Mercy looked up at it a bit too eagerly. It was alone though, not the flock she had befriended yesterday. Her heart sped a little faster. Surely they would show up? There was still time.

Mercy maneuvered her way to the front of the

crowd. The outer wall of the pub was where they were going to line up Thomas and Andrei for the firing squad. Several hunters were clearing people from the area, and that was where everyone gathered.

A spark of rage ignited in her. How dare they choose to murder them in front of her mother's pub! She balled her hands into fists, feeling her pulse quicken and pound in her temples. No, this wasn't the time or the place to get mad. They would soon be run out of town. Possibly even killed. She took deep breaths and tried to calm herself.

Applause slowly grew from the direction of the jail, rising to a roar as a crowd of people clustered around the commotion.

Mercy's heart sank as the people came into view. Thomas was in front, trotting quickly with his hands tied behind his back. He had a large black eye and his hands were bloody behind him from the friction of the ropes. He also ran with a limp on bare feet. His normally brilliant fiery red hair clung limply to his head and his eyes were sunken and heavy. Mercy swallowed down her panic and watched as Sheriff Barlow pushed him up against the wall.

Thomas had clearly been tortured and hadn't been given basic care for his wounds. He stumbled at one point and the sheriff had to go lift him up and lean him against the wall.

"I didn't expect to see you here."

Mercy wanted to scream when she realized someone was talking to her. She bit her tongue to stay calm, tasting blood in her mouth.

Familiar white hair and tired eyes met hers. "Doctor Keene!"

He gave a sad smile. "I am truly sorry you have to see this." He dropped his eyes. "This city has changed horribly over the last ten years. And you—" He lowered his voice. "You can't even step outside without hiding."

Doctor Keene knew who she was. He knew who she was, even in this disguise in the middle of the largest crowd of hunters ever gathered in Kanta. Panic erupted in her chest, but she pushed it down, trying to figure out what to do.

Another round of applause lifted in the distance.

Andrei.

She glanced at her people mixed in with the crowd, mind running through all the possibilities. They weren't supposed to attack civilians, but Mercy had seen enough scrapes to know accidents happened. People got hurt. Doctor Keene wasn't on her do-not-harm list she had given everyone. She had honestly completely forgotten about him until this moment.

She leaned up and whispered into his ear, "This is about to get really bad. I need you to get out of here."

His face went pale and his mouth dropped open. "Mercy?" he whispered.

"Go to the mill and let yourself inside. You can hide in one of the grinders if you have to. Just stay low and I'll come and get you."

She pulled away. He stared at her with a mixture of fear and confusion. "But—"

"No time for questions, just go!" she hissed, giving him a light push.

He backed away, nodded quickly, then ran off. She looked around to see a few people looking at her, possibly suspicious or insulted, thinking she just threatened the town physician. She wasn't sure if it was enough to keep him safe, but she had to hope it would be.

The applause reached her, then surrounded her, and her eyes fell on Andrei. Suddenly, the air seemed to get sucked out of her lungs. He glanced in her direction—her heart raced in her chest—then he turned back to look at the path ahead of him. The look in his eyes was heartbreaking. Like he still had hope, like he expected Mercy to be standing there with a rifle on her back and taking out the sheriff. She was here; she wanted to tell him. She hadn't abandoned him, but she couldn't tell him.

Andrei looked like he hadn't slept in days. Dried blood stained his shoulder and a nasty gash looked fresh down the side of his cheek. He had no shoes and was clearly in pain as he kept up the quick pace prodded by Lieutenant Hastings at the point of his rifle. It took everything in Mercy's being not to put her hand to her mouth, to scream, to wail, to cry out—to do anything that a normal grieving person might want to do for someone they loved facing a firing squad.

This was another piece Kanta had stolen from her, another emotion she was denied. As Andrei was shoved against the wall, stumbled to his knees, and pulled back up again, the crowd cheered, but Mercy was snarling. She cried out, not out of excitement like the others, but out of rage. Just a fraction of the steam she had kept bottled up inside for too long.

More applause erupted from the entrance of the pub. The firing squad emerged from the front door. It looked like several of them had already been drinking. They were smiling and laughing, waving at the crowd as though they were celebrities.

Her hand hovered over the holstered gun on her hip, already unsnapped and loaded, ready for firing. Just as she was about to pull it out and start taking shots, a crow cawed.

Mercy looked up at the clear blue sky and saw the flock of crows drifting on the breeze. As the sheriff spoke with the firing squad and the lieutenant tied Andrei and Thomas to pipes along the wall, the flock landed. Some went to the roof of the pub, others to the ground near where Thomas and Andrei stood. Some more landed on the ground behind the crowd. To the crowd it probably looked like scavengers come to feast on the bodies after the shooting stopped, but to Mercy it was like seeing a welcome old friend again. She had tears in her eyes as they lighted on the wooden rooftops and scuttled across the ground.

"Out of the way, you flea-bitten vermin!" Lieutenant Hastings kicked at one of the crows. His boot didn't land, but Mercy tensed. The lieutenant would be killed first.

The firing squad lined up. Six shooters had assembled for the two men and looked like they had been pulled from various parts of town. Probably asked to volunteer. They would regret that decision.

The sheriff got up beside where the firing squad was setting up, reading off a few papers. "Welcome, everyone, to Kanta's first public execution. I understand such events haven't happened in the past, but today is a new day! Now it may have taken some suggestions to get the judge on our side, but I reckon it wasn't too hard of a task."

He waved to a man standing beside the entrance of the pub, a tall man with a crooked smile, pink skin, and holding a giant mug of ale in one hand.

The judge waved back at the sheriff with a drunken laugh. "Anytime!" he cried with a wide grin.

The crowd laughed. Mercy grit her teeth. That would be number two.

"Now, today we're killing off two men who have apparently been swindling the people of Kanta for some time. First up: Thomas Farrell."

The crowd booed. Some threw rotten vegetables at him. One potato hit him hard on his leg. If he hadn't been tied to the pipe, he would have fallen hard to the ground.

"Anything you want to say, Thomas?" the sheriff sneered.

"Yes, actually, I—"

"Now that I think about it," the sheriff laughed, cutting him off. "I don't think he has anything useful to say."

The entire crowd laughed, all except for Mercy's people, who looked on with rage. Mercy dug her nails into her palms until it hurt.

"Next up," the sheriff continued, "We have Andrei.

Thomas' assistant and fellow swindler. Anything you want to add, boy?"

Andrei looked at the ground, shoulders rounded, as if he was completely broken inside. He didn't even lift his head up at the question. Mercy wanted to rush over there, hug him, and tell him it would be alright. Instead, she had to watch as people threw old, moldy squash at his head. One hit him in the face, slid slowly down, and left behind a gross stain on his cheek. He looked about to cry.

"How dare he!" someone yelled out from the crowd.

Andrei's eyes went wide. "Mr. Gently?"

"That's right!" An old man hobbled up to the sheriff, holding a cane over his head. "Andrei used to work for me at the apothecary. Once upon a time, I thought he was a good man, an incredibly kind employee. I found out his entire family was killed by werewolves, but it seems that wasn't entirely true. Andrei has been alive this entire time, stealing from good, honest people like me." He spat on the ground near Andrei's bare feet. "I hope he rots!"

Andrei hung his head to his chest and bawled, shaking from head to toe. Fat tears rolled down his cheeks. Mercy felt another cry rising up, but she pushed it down.

The sheriff shoved Mr. Gently away from the firing range, and the crowd parted, helping direct the old man away from the stage. Finally the sheriff turned to the firing squad, clearing his throat.

"Ready, men?"

They nodded in agreement, shouldering their rifles

one by one. The sheriff raised a hand into the air. A hush fell over the crowd and the hairs on the back of Mercy's neck stood up.

"Now!" she cried.

In an instant, everything around her shifted.

PART 6

11

CACOPHONY

NO SOONER DID the words leave Mercy's mouth, then every crow in the street flew into the air in a great swirling mass. People around her jumped, some cowered, and others stared at the birds in confusion. All stared at them as they flew into the brilliant blue sky at once and began their quick descent.

The birds were a distraction.

At the entrance of the pub, Rose jumped from around the corner of the building, wrapped a hand over the judge's mouth, and dragged him back into an alleyway. Leyda caught Mercy's eye and gave her a nod. The judge's eyes were wide as he disappeared.

The crows began their assault on the crowd, pecking at hands, clawing at faces, and then flying into the sky again. The crowd gathered to watch her friends be killed was now screaming and running around in panic.

Seeing the birds were handling themselves without help, Mercy turned her sights to the lieutenant, the jerk who had hurt her Andrei just minutes before. Like the others, he stared at the birds with eyes wide and mouth gaping. He was also working to pull the gun out of his hip holster.

Did he plan to shoot Andrei and Thomas anyway? Or did he intend to shoot at her bird friends? Either way, Mercy saw red. She growled and lunged forward, her gun tight in her grip. She dodged out of the way of a man crying on the ground as two crows pecked at the back of his shirt. An older woman had been knocked to the ground as the crowd scrambled to get away from the birds. People ran beside her, but she didn't move. Across her waist was a satchel of more moldy squashes. Mercy tore her gaze away from the woman and focused again on the lieutenant.

He had his gun aimed up at the sky, trying to take aim, but the birds were too fast for him.

Mercy stopped in her tracks and lifted her gun. Remembering her training, she let out a slow breath, blocking out the screams, the panic, and the chaos surrounding her. Just as she was preparing to pull the trigger, the lieutenant looked up and met her gaze. For a brief instant, doubt crept into her heart and she questioned. She hesitated. Was this right? Should she kill him?

The lieutenant swung his arm toward her, and the doubt disappeared. Mercy pulled the trigger once, then again.

Just like it had years ago, the explosive sound of bullet propelled by gunpowder drowned out everything else, leaving her arms sore and her ears ringing.

With wide-eyed horror, the lieutenant put a hand to

his chest. Crimson blossomed on his grungy off-white shirt. Blood dribbled out the corner of his mouth and he stumbled and fell to the ground.

Mercy allowed herself the luxury of a smile. She glanced toward Andrei and Thomas. Both were on their knees, trying to stay low as bullets flew through the air. Each of them had a small team of crows working to tear through the thick ropes binding their hands behind them.

Andrei caught her gaze and Mercy gave him a short nod before turning away. Her heart swelled.

Good. They had to be confused and horrified, but at least they would be free soon. Then they could take proper cover and not get hurt in the madness of the fight.

Pain burst on the left side of Mercy's head, like a fire put to her ear, burning out everything else around her. Warmth pooled onto her shoulder and Mercy fell hard to her knees. A hand to her head came back coated in crimson.

No, this wasn't supposed to be how it ended. She was supposed to see Andrei, to hug him and tell him he would be alright. They were supposed to take back Kanta together. They were supposed to be happy.

The bandanna around her mouth soaked through and sank down her face as she breathed hard. It nestled warm beneath her chin against her throat. Pain throbbed in her skull as her hearing returned, pulse pounding endlessly in her ears. It sounded like a war zone with guns firing everywhere. Something hot pressed to the tender skin of her neck and she flinched back instinctively.

Towering over her, his rifle held out before him and aimed at her neck, stood Sheriff Barlow.

He had narrow, calculating eyes and a sneer on his lips. His brow glistened with sweat as the sneer turned upward into a smirk. He lifted up the rifle and knocked her hat off of her head. Her hair fell around her face. Mercy winced.

"You're nothing but a little girl," he said with such derision that Mercy shook with outrage.

"Not a little girl," she said, clenching her teeth against the pain.

He arched his eyebrows.

"I am a Wolf of Kanta."

He laughed loud and shook his head, sliding the barrel of the gun against her neck again. "Is that right?"

Mercy glared at him.

"You would be dead already if my bullet hadn't grazed you like that. Not much of a wolf if you're dead, are you, child?"

Mercy reached one hand down to her waist and felt the dagger Kit had given her, the one she hadn't had reason to even pull out until now.

"Drop the gun, little girl. Time to stop playing with the big boys." He looked her up and down. "Shame about those scars on your face. Without those, you would have made a nice little sum, as pretty as you are."

A growl came to her throat, but Mercy pushed it down with some effort. She dropped the gun, knowing the sheriff would shoot her if she didn't. The blood from her head wound had dripped down her shirt and onto her belt. The handle of the knife was covered with it. She couldn't grip it well enough to pull it out of the sheath. It was too slippery.

"Come on, now. On your feet. I don't want to be left empty-handed. I deserve some compensation after the stunt you and your trained birds played today."

Mercy looked around at the people who had been trampled on the ground, to the many people around her running and screaming, and to the crows still attacking people en masse.

Where were her friends? Why weren't they here at her side to help her? Because they were also trying to survive, she reminded herself. The two officers weren't the only ones to bring guns, based on all the gunshots she was hearing. She needed to take the sheriff out on her own. No guns, no chemicals, and without relying on others. It had to be done by hand, by herself, and it had to be done now.

The sheriff cocked the rifle. "Don't make me ask again. I don't like disobedient children."

Finally the blade handle settled in her hand and she pulled it from the sheath. A growl rose out of her like a shriek. Mercy pushed off with her back foot and shoved the rifle to the side. The sheriff pulled the trigger, but the gunshot went off to the side, into the ground. But it was too late. The terror in his eyes said he knew it too. He leaned back, trying to get distance between them, to get the rifle around in front of him again. But Mercy's powerful growl put him off balance, shaken and alarmed. She pulled her hand back and stabbed the knife into his throat. He gave a gurgling gasp as she shoved him down onto the ground. Another shot burst into the sky before she knocked the rifle out of his hand.

His pupils were pinpricks as she removed the blade, and crimson gushed out of him in pulses timed with his slowing heart. She leaned forward, her lips mere inches away from his ear.

"I am a Wolf of Kanta. We are mad and we are many." When she pulled back, she saw his lips moving, but no sound came out. The puddle of blood around him grew larger, and soon he stopped breathing.

Shaking from head to toe, Mercy climbed off of the dead man. A part of her was horrified, but another part of her wanted to celebrate killing the man who had almost killed her family. Her pulse pounded violently in her temples and Mercy felt like her head weighed double. Walking straight was difficult.

All around Main Street were scuffles, but she didn't hear gunshots as often as she had before. Mostly she saw partially and fully transformed werewolves stalking hunters down in broad daylight.

To her weary eyes, it looked like they had won. She reached up and tore off the bloody bandanna, feeling the wind against her face in public for the first time in years. She didn't fear existing here, not any longer. She wanted to take up space without fearing for her life or her freedom. Such a simple joy to be denied for so long by such disgusting people.

"Mercy!"

Her heart skipped a beat. She knew that voice, had dreamed of it for months. Her imagination could never match its particular tenor, the waver in his voice, or the emotion that filled every syllable. Just hearing his joy again after missing it for so long sent her stomach tumbling.

Andrei's arms were around her suddenly, hugging, holding, touching. He held her chin in his hand and pressed his beautiful lips against hers. She kissed him back, melted against him, and savored his cracked and bruised lips. How many times had she dreamed of this, hoped for this? All those late nights under Oscar's watch, she scripted what she would say or do when she finally saw him again. Instead, all she could do was hold him, kiss him, and cry ugly tears.

It felt perfect in every way.

"I don't know how you did it, but you saved us," Andrei said, breathless. "I honestly thought we were dead."

Thomas limped up to stand near them, rubbing at his wounded wrists.

Mercy pulled away from Andrei and gave Thomas a hug. "I'm glad you're okay!"

Thomas gave her a lopsided smile. "I am too. I admit, I wasn't sure if we would be." He sniffed and wiped at his good eye.

Mercy went back to Andrei, wrapping her arms around his neck, and he put his hands on her hips, smiling. She never wanted to be separated again. "I didn't do it on my own."

Thomas cocked an eyebrow at her. "Who helped exactly? I don't recognize those werewolves back there."

"Kit, Rose, Leyda, and I put our heads together and

figured out what to do." Mercy shook her head. "Honestly, I'm surprised it worked out at all."

"Wait a minute," Andrei said, a cute smirk on his lips. "You're telling me you and Leyda worked together without killing each other? I'm impressed."

She nudged him playfully. "Don't be. I've changed, you know. I've grown a lot."

His expression shifted to bittersweet. "Yeah, I guess we all have."

Above Main Street, the crows swarmed in an ever-shifting mass. Mercy hoped none of them were killed in the fight, but she had almost been killed too.

"Thank you," she muttered and nodded her head to the birds.

Andrei looked at her in confusion. "Mercy, what?"

In a flash, the flock of crows shifted direction and flew straight toward them.

Thomas took a step back, his arms out to the side as if ready to sprint if needed. Beside her, Andrei tensed as if ready to run too.

"Uh… Mercy?"

She squeezed him tight. "It's okay. Just hug me. They're friends of mine."

Worry etched into his face. "You sure?"

She smiled and gave him a brief kiss. "Trust me."

He took a deep breath before holding her tight and burying his head against her shoulder. The swarm of birds swept across them like a cacophony. All sound was replaced with the beating of wings and their intense caws. The wind swept her hair as they passed and she felt their feathers graze her face and arms.

Still holding onto her tightly, Andrei was trembling. Mercy smiled. He had so much to learn, and she would have to teach him.

She truly had grown so much since she had first met him. She hoped together they would grow even more.

12

A NEW START

MERCY STACKED the beakers onto the bloated wooden tray, attempting to keep them from toppling when she had to carry them upstairs. She needed to replace the tray, but she hadn't had the time.

Ever since Kanta became a werewolf sanctuary, and Mercy no longer had to hide herself or her work, demand for her cure had only risen. Farrell Mill wasn't suited for constant production, but the newly abandoned apothecary was.

Mercy balanced the tray with one hand, leaning it against her hip as she headed for the stairs. The boards creaked and gave under her weight. Mr. Gently hadn't upgraded the place in many years and the stairs were number one on Thomas' repair list… once he was fully recovered and started the business with the mill again. It would take time for him to make a profit, and that was fine by her. It gave her time to adjust to this new life, this new home.

Honestly, Mercy could deal with warped steps. She

had dealt with far worse over the past few months and it felt silly to fret over stairs. Still, she always kept a free hand so she could grip the banister just in case. The jars clinked as she went up to the main shop floor.

"It's looking so good! I didn't know you knew anything about running an apothecary," Rose beamed.

"I'm... still learning." Andrei said. "I was only an assistant before. I was hoping Mr. Gently would want to stay and help teach me the ropes, at least, but he called me a fugitive."

Rose scoffed. "He was going to put innocent people to death. He's hardly guilt free, either."

Andrei gave a nervous laugh.

Mercy's heart broke for him. She knew how much he hated how everything fell apart with Mr. Gently. They had long conversations each night about it. He would still cry about it sometimes, even though it had been a week ago. Mr. Gently was one of the people who had reminded Andrei of his past life, of his family. Mercy hated that the druggist had let him down. Andrei had thought of him as a surrogate father at one point in his life. But Mr. Gently had been monstrous in his own right. It didn't help that Rose didn't always pick up Andrei's subtle social cues and tended to push when she needed to back down.

Mercy decided to be a distraction.

"Breakable glass, coming through! Stay clear, everybody!"

The main floor of the apothecary was a large rectangular room with shelves along the walls. Various tonics, balms, and ointments lined the shelves. The front windows displayed their primary items: large jars of Mercy's partial vaccine, complete with signs and professional labels. It was easily their most popular item, and they tried to sell it as cheaply as possible so anyone could help themselves or a loved one.

Mercy pushed the wooden tray onto one of the glass display shelves and the contents of the jars glittered in the morning sun.

"Glad to see you two catching up." Mercy glanced at the cashier counter to see Andrei's appreciative smile. "How is Leyda doing?"

"Much better," Rose said, nerves audible in her voice. "Thomas has been working with her. Says she needs more physical therapy still. I'm heading over to get lunch with her in a minute. I just finished bringing back Silver and Jamison from the house and wanted to check out the progress on the shop. I'm always seeing people come in and out. Now I see why!"

Andrei put his hands in his pockets. "It's been a lot of work. And I am way over my head here, but once upon a time I talked with a lovely friend about what we would do together someday."

Mercy smiled.

"I guess it was the obvious choice for both of us." He put a hand to his chest. "I'm just lucky I'm dating a genius."

Heat rose to Mercy's cheeks. "Okay, that's enough, Andrei." She turned to continue stocking the shelves.

He laughed, and Mercy couldn't help but grin. She never got tired of hearing his beautiful laugh.

"I've got to get going." Rose headed for the door. "Be good, you two lovebirds."

Mercy rolled her eyes as Rose left. She made her way over to the cashier counter with a laugh. "She's ridiculous sometimes."

He furrowed his brows. "I meant what I said, you know. I am lucky to have you. And you are a genius."

She sighed, making her way behind the counter. "When you say things like that, it does things to me."

"Oh?" He feigned surprise.

She nodded. "Especially in that vest and button-up shirt. You look nice all cleaned up."

He narrowed his eyes. "Don't worry. I can be more wolfish later."

Mercy quickly closed the gap between them. When he bantered like that, she couldn't help herself. She pressed her lips against his and smirked at his little gasp of surprise.

She pulled back, straightening down the collar on his shirt. "I love you, you know that?"

"Of course I do. You're not exactly subtle."

She chuckled.

He pulled her into an embrace. "I love you too. I don't want to ever be separated like that from you again."

She met his warm brown eyes. "You won't have to. I'm not going anywhere."

Slipping a hand around his neck, she pulled him into another kiss, deeper, more passionate.

She wished this moment could last forever, wiping away all the painful memories and nightmares. Taking away all their loss and sorrow. She wanted to kiss away his pain, his fears, his regrets.

The bell rang at the front door.

She pulled away, smiling at Andrei's flush.

"It's a customer," he said simply.

Mercy loved this man more than anything. She held him a moment longer, savoring in the feel of him. She never wanted to let him go again, but he did have a customer.

EPILOGUE

IT WAS A HOT, windy climb to the top of the roof. Even at night, the summer heat never seemed to abate. Mercy was glad she had her working gloves to wear because the rungs of the ladder were hot enough to burn.

When she got to the top, she stretched her hands and looked around, spotting Kit on the front end of the roof near Main Street overlooking Kanta. Leyda was right, Kit was hiding up here.

"Kit! Are you okay?"

She lay on her back, arms behind her head, staring up at the starry sky. "Oh, hey."

Mercy walked up to her, trying not to be worried about how casually Kit was acting. "Um, you do know it's night, right?"

"Yep," Kit said.

Mercy blinked at her. "So, why are you out here alone? Everybody is freaking out below. Thomas has torn the entire mill apart looking for you. Dr. Keene was trying to check on his leg, but Thomas decided to turn it into a scavenger hunt."

She gave an annoyed sigh. "I told him I needed to think."

"You do know that werewolves are out at night, right?"

She was quiet a moment before she responded tersely, "And you know we haven't had a werewolf attack here in months. I'm on the roof of the tallest building in Kanta. I'm fine."

This wasn't like Kit. She didn't usually lose her temper so easily, especially when her safety was involved. Mercy sat down beside her, pulling her knees to her chest. A warm breeze swept across the rooftop, making Mercy's blouse billow. In the distance, she could make out the new homes being built. Kanta was growing quickly, and people were clamoring for protection from the dangers that preyed on the rest of the world. Many came to Kanta with a host of skills from their old lives. They had a new grocer, hotel manager, and even a sheriff who was in the process of a total revamp of the jail to make it more humane. It was the beginning of a tenuous new world. One Mercy hoped would lead to wonderful, new perspectives. But it was only a beginning.

"Do you remember your dad?" Kit asked.

Mercy was pulled from her thoughts. "Yes," she said, uncertainly.

"I saw your mother's painting at the apothecary yesterday. She was really pretty."

"I know." Mercy hugged her knees, remembering how Rose and Andrei helped her hang it up.

Kit was quiet for a long time, but the silence was pregnant with a question that hadn't been asked. Clearly Kit wasn't in the mood to be pushed, so Mercy waited and watched the stars in the sky, the full moon illuminating the world below. She listened to the wind howl against the mill and the ebb and flow of the crickets in the forest below. Finally, she couldn't deal with the silence any longer.

"Why are you really up here, Kit?" she asked. "And if you say stargazing, that's not true, and we both know it."

Kit let out a shaky breath. "I want to find my mom."

The hairs went up on the back of Mercy's neck. "But Kit, she was captured by traffickers. Just like you."

"I know," she said in a flat voice. "I want to find out what happened to her. I want to know who my father is, where I come from. I... can't remember what she looks like any longer and it scares me. But I know I'll recognize her if I see her."

Mercy reached over and put a hand on her shoulder. "I'm sorry."

Kit was silent for a long moment and Mercy asked what she felt was an obvious if difficult question.

"What if she's dead, Kit?"

She turned to look at her, her eyes glassy from crying. "Then I want to make sure she is dead. I want to make sure she isn't suffering like you and Rose did with Oscar. I want to save her. You understand, don't you?"

Mercy understood. It was the same reason she had

taken her mother's portrait home from her childhood home, despite knowing Oscar had painted it. She wanted a piece of her mother, some small fraction of her life, no matter how ephemeral. She wanted some way to know a woman who had been a big part of her life. "I understand completely," she said.

Kit bit her lip. "Do you think I can do it? On my own?"

Mercy blinked at her. "On your own? Why would you do that? It's too dangerous."

Kit stared at her with glassy eyes. They carried an intensity that took Mercy off guard.

"You've thought about this a long time, haven't you?" Mercy asked.

She nodded. "I think I know generally what town she was in. I could get Andrei to drop me off at where I think she is. Give me a couple of days, then pick me up again. He's always doing deliveries anyway. It won't be too far out of his way. I promise I won't be a bother."

Mercy shook her head. "You are never a bother."

"Listen, can you talk to Thomas? I don't want him freaking out. You know how protective he can be. I… I need to do this, Mercy. On my own. If I go searching with a whole team, I might never find her. It might put her in danger, or make her go underground."

Mercy sighed, climbing to her feet. "I don't know."

Kit sat up in a flash and grabbed Mercy's hand, squeezing it tight, her skin chilly in the warm night air. "Please. I never ask for anything. Just this." Tears fell down her cheeks. "I need to know if she's alive, Mercy, before she dies or disappears completely. If I don't do this, I may never find out anything."

She slid a hand over Kit's, giving it a squeeze. "Okay, I'll arrange it. But if you run into any trouble, you send a crow. See if you can get one to follow you. Any sign of trouble and the bird leads me straight back to you. Understood?"

"Thank you, Mercy!" Kit was on her feet and wrapping her arms around her in a tight embrace. "Thank you for believing in me."

Mercy stared up at the stars and the ever watching full moon, hoping she had made the right decision.

She didn't want to be held responsible for sending Kit to her death, but she also knew she had no right to stop her either. Kit was her own person, and she chose the path she wanted to take.

Regardless of the dangers that awaited her.

AFTERWORD

It's been a little over a year since I started releasing The Wolves of Kanta series, starting with the revamped edition of The She-Wolf of Kanta. I set out to do a rapid release of a five book series, continuing Mercy's journey and building on the world I created years ago, starting with the rerelease of She-Wolf. It's been both a challenge and a privilege to create this series, book by book. I'm so incredibly proud of closing it where I wanted to, of how far Mercy has come, and of how Kanta has been transformed by Mercy's actions.

I always knew that the end of the series would require Kanta to change, and by extension, the world around them. There's no way the werewolf sanctuary would go unnoticed by others. Mercy has literally upheaved the landscape. I hope to explore this more in Kit's upcoming storyline.

Kit will get her own series where she will search for her mother in the world outside of Kanta, and maybe find clues to the strange behavior of the werewolves that Mercy couldn't explain. I hope you'll return to join me again when Kit's spin-off series releases!

ALSO BY MARLENA FRANK

The Stolen Series

Young adult, portal fantasy, faeries

Stolen

Broken

Chosen

The Wolves of Kanta Series

Young adult, dark fantasy, steampunk, werewolves

The She-Wolf of Kanta

The Blood of Kanta

The Hunters of Kanta

The Fury of Kanta

The Howl of Kanta

Monstrous Creatures Series

Young adult, horror, sci-fi, dystopian

The Seeking

Ominous Hour Series

Horror, short stories, standalone

A Beautiful Specimen

Undertow

Standalone

Short stories, horror, dark fantasy
The Impostor and Other Dark Tales

Weird western, werewolves, vampires, short story
Night Feeders

Mystery, film noir, humor, short story
The Mysterious Disappearance of Charlene Kerringer

summon Death to help them, but Death is not easily swayed. Neither of the sisters are prepared for the consequences.

Want a peek behind the scenes?
Want to preview my books before they get released?

Get exclusive access to book goodies, giveaways, and cover reveals by joining my mailing list. Not only will you get notified of all my new releases, you'll get an exclusive copy of The Blade Filled with Stars.

Subscribe to the Mailing List at:
http://marlenafrank.com/mailinglist/

Follow me on Ko-Fi for regular updates on my writing progress.

Monthly subscribers get access to sneak peeks at stories way before anyone else. They also get access to cover reveals, monthly shout-outs on social media, and thanked by name in the acknowledgements in my books.

http://ko-fi.com/MarlenaFrank

ACKNOWLEDGMENTS

The Howl of Kanta was a collaborative book, like all the books in this series have been. I've been privileged to have the help of many artists, authors, and editors throughout my writing process. So I have a long list of people to thank.

Lara Zielinsky has been the editor for almost the entire series. Her keen eye and incredibly helpful feedback has helped to shape the characters, the world, and also my prose. She has a wonderful way of giving feedback without changing the meaning behind my words, which I appreciate immensely. I hope to work with her again on my future projects.

Harvest Moon Designs did incredible work with the cover, as they did with all the books in this series. Not only did they go through a lengthy process for each book cover, taking all of my input and ideas into consideration, but they were also incredibly prompt and their work is absolutely beautiful!

My sister, Kelley M. Frank of Morbid Smile Art, did a wonderful job with the map for this series. She has also been an incredible help throughout the writing of these books, giving me regular feedback and support. I was more than happy to hire her for the lovely interior illustrations that help separate the parts in this book. For the last book in this series, I wanted something different. She not only understood what I wanted, but created the beautiful artwork you see in here. I'm in awe of her skill and appreciate her help as always!

A special thanks to my parents, who are always incredibly supportive of my work and are there to help in any way they can. They have always been so helpful to me in my creative journey and I'm so grateful to them. A big thanks to my Aunt Charmaine for always being there for me and supporting my writing in any way she can.

Two of my author friends, Candace Robinson and Carla Lewis, have been pillars of support to me throughout the writing of this series. They have cheered me on, encouraged me, and been a sympathetic ear throughout the writing of this series, as they have been with all of my projects.

Thank you to Donna, my incredibly supportive monthly Ko-Fi supporter, for your continued support throughout the writing of this series! She is a friend and a constant reader who is so helpful with all the things we chat about over on my Ko-Fi.

Finally, thank you to my readers. This series would never have been revitalized without your help! I am so grateful that you joined me here with Mercy. I hope you'll come back to the world of Kanta again to explore Kit's tale as well. Thank you for your support!

ABOUT THE AUTHOR

Marlena Frank is the author of young adult fantasy and horror novels, short stories, novellas, and book series. Many of her books have hit the bestseller charts, including her debut novel, Stolen. Her work has been praised by Readers' Favorite and featured in De Mode of Literature Magazine. Her stories have appeared in anthologies such as Emporium of Superstition, Catstruck!, Heroic Fantasy Quarterly, Georgia Gothic, and The Sirens Call ezine.

Although born in Tennessee, Marlena has spent most of her life in Georgia. She lives with her sister and two spoiled adopted cats. She serves as the Vice President of the Atlanta Chapter of the Horror Writers Association, is an active member of the Science Fiction and Fantasy Writers Association, and is an avid member of the Atlanta cosplay community.

She is also an INFJ, a tea drinker, and a wildlife enthusiast.

Support her on Ko-Fi: ko-fi.com/MarlenaFrank
Follow her at: MarlenaFrank.com

www.ingramcontent.com/pod-product-compliance
Lightning Source LLC
Chambersburg PA
CBHW011558190726
48287CB00010B/2951